WOODCUTS
OF
WOMEN

Also by Dagoberto Gilb

The Magic of Blood
The Last Known Residence of Mickey Acuña

WOODCUTS

OF
WOMEN

Dagoberto Gilb

GROVE PRESS
New York

Published simultaneously in Canada
Printed in the United States of America

FIRST EDITION

Library of Congress Cataloging-in-Publication Data

Gilb, Dagoberto, 1950–
    Woodcuts of women/Dagoberto Gilb.— 1st ed.
        p. cm.
    Contents: Maria de Covina — Mayela one day in 1989 — Hueco — Shout — The pillows — About Tere who was in Palomas — Brisa —A painting in Sante Fe — Bottoms — Snow.
    ISBN 0-8021-1679-5
    1. Mexican American women — Fiction. 2. Southwestern States — Social life and customs — Fiction. I. Title.

PS3557.I296 W6 2001
813'.54 — dc21   00-060060

Design by Julie Duquet

GROVE PRESS
841 Broadway
New York, NY 10003

01 02 03 04   10 9 8 7 6 5 4 3 2 1

as a prayer
for love
to be forgiven

Acknowledgments

The author wishes to thank the Mrs. Giles Whiting Foundation and John Simon Guggenheim Foundation for their generous financial support.

Also thanks to friends (a random ordering) who have provided their friendship at moments they are not even aware of, who have tolerated and encouraged me for years: William Timberman, the late Ricardo Sánchez, Rick DeMarinis, Annie Proulx, Ixchel Rosal, Armando Villareal, George Keating, Paige Martinez, Elizabeth Hadas, Tish Hinojosa, Francisco Goldman, Elena Castedo, Wendy Lesser, Oscar Casares, Pat Carr, Pat Little Dog, Hettie Jones—and Judy Hottensen, and Morgan Entrekin.

Grateful acknowledgment is made to the following magazines where these stories first appeared: *The New Yorker*, "Maria de Covina"; *Ploughshares*, "Mayela One Day in 1989," "The Pillows"; *DoubleTake*, "Hueco"; *The Threepenny Review*, "About Tere Who Was in Palomas"; *New Dog*, "Brisa"; *The Texas Observer*, "A Painting in Santa Fe."

Contents

WOODCUTS
OF
WOMEN

Maria de Covina

I've got two sports coats, about six ties, three dressy pants, Florsheims I polish *a la madre,* and three weeks ago I bought a suit, with silk lining, at Lemonde for Men. It came with a matching vest. That's what made it for me. I love getting all duded up, looking fine, I really do. This is the thing: I like women. No, wait. I *love* women. I know that don't sound like anything new, nothing every guy wouldn't tell you. I mean it though, and it's that I can't say so better. It's not like I do anything different when I'm around them. I'm not like aggressive, going after them, hustling. I don't play that. I don't do anything except have a weakness for them. I don't ask anybody out. I already have my girlfriend Diana. Still, it's like I feel drunk around them. Like they make me so *pedo* I can't move away. See what I'm saying? So yeah, of course I love working nights at The Broadway. Women's perfume is everywhere, and I'm dizzy while I'm there.

Even if what I'm about to say might not sound right, I'm saying it: It's not just me, it's them too, it's them *back,* maybe even first. Okay, I realize this sounds bad, so I won't talk about it. But why else did they put me in the Gifts department? I didn't know *ni nada* about that stuff, and I noticed right away that most customers were women. And I'm not meaning to brag, but the truth is I sell, they buy. They're older women almost always, rich I see now, because the things we have on the racks —*cositas como* vases and statues and baskets and bowls, from Russia, Germany, Africa, Denmark, France, Argentina, everywhere— are originals and they're expensive. These ladies, maybe they're older, but a lot really look good for being older, they come in and they ask my opinion. They're smiling when they ask me what I'd like if it was for me. I try to be honest. I smile a lot. I smile because I'm happy.

You know what? Even if I'm wrong, *no le hace,* I don't care. Because when I go down the escalator, right at the bottom is Cindy in Cosmetics. She says, "Is your mommy coming for you tonight?" Cindy's almost blond, very pretty, and way out there. She leans over the glass to get close to me. She wears her blouses a little low-cut. She's big for being such a *flaquita.*

"Maybe," I say. "Maybe not."

"Don't marry her yet." That bedroom voice of hers.

"What difference will it make?"

"None to me," she says.

"You talk big," I say, "but do you walk the walk?"

"You know where I am. What're we waiting for?"

She's not wrong. I'm the one who only talks the talk. I don't lie to myself. For instance, I'm about to be nineteen, but I pretend I'm twenty. I do get away with it. I pass for older. I'm not sure why that's true—since I'm thirteen I've had a job—or why I want it to be. I feel older when I say I am. For the same reason I let them think I know so much about sex. *Ya sabes,* pretend that I'm all experienced, like I'm all bad. Lots of girls, and that I know what they like. I feel like it's true when I'm around them. It's what Cindy thinks. And I want her to, I like it that she does, but at the same time it makes me scared of her. She's not pretending, and I'm afraid she'll find out about me: The truth is that my only experience is with Diana. I'm too embarrassed to admit it, and I don't, even to her.

It's not just Cindy though, and this isn't talk, and though it might sound like it, honest, I'm not trying to brag. Over in Women's Fashions is Ana, a *morena* with green eyes, and strong, pretty legs. She's shy. Not that shy. She wants to be in love, wants a wedding, wants a baby. In Housewares is Brigit. Brigit is Russian, and sometimes she's hard to understand. You should see her. She's got the bones of a black girl, but her skin is snow. I think she's older than she looks. She'll go out with me, I know it. I don't know how she'd be, and I wonder. Over there, down the mall, at Lemonde for Men, is where Liz works. That's who I bought my suit from. Liz is fun. Likes to laugh. The Saturday I picked up my suit we had lunch together, and then one night, when I knew she was working, just before we closed, I called her. I told her I was hungry and would she want to go somewhere after. She said yeah. We only kissed good-bye. The next time she was letting me feel her. She likes it, and she's not embarrassed that she does. I think about her a lot. Touching her. But I don't want this to sound so *gacho*, porno or something. I like her, that's what I mean. I like everything about her. I don't know how to say it better.

"You're such a liar," Maria says. She's my boss. The assistant manager of Gifts and Luggage, Silverware and China. I worry that she knows how old I really am, and she's going by that. Or that she knows I'm not really going to college in the day. I don't know why I can't be honest about having that other job. I work for A-Tron Monday through Friday during the day. A shipping clerk. It's a good job too. But it's better to say you're studying for something better. I am going to go to college next year, after I save some money.

"What're you saying?"

"You just want to get them," Maria de Covina says. "You're no different than any other man."

I have told her a lot, I'm not sure why. Probably because she catches me all the time talking to them. The first times I thought

5

she was getting mad and going around checking up on me because I'd be on a break and taking too long. But she's cool. We just seemed to run into each other a lot, and she would like shake her head at me, so now I tell her how I'm thinking. I told her about Liz after she saw us on that first Saturday, eating lunch in the mall.

"It's not true," I say.

"It's not *true*," she whines. She often repeats what I say in a mocking voice. Sometimes she gets close to me, and this time she gets real close, close enough to reach her hand around and grab one of my *nalgas*. "It's not *true*."

"Watch it, Covina," I say. "You Italians think everything you squeeze is a soft *tomate*, but Mexicans got *chiles* that burn."

I call her Maria de Covina because she lives in West Covina and drives in. I call her Italian because she doesn't know a word of Spanish, and Italians can be named Maria. I can't let up. She really is Mexican American, just the spoiled, *pocha* princess type. But I don't let on. She tells me her last name over and over. What do you think Mata is? she asks. Does *Mata* sound Italian to you? I say maybe, yeah. Like a first name like Maria, I say. Like a last name like Corona. Probably it's that, I tell her, and you're messing with me. I don't understand yet what you're up to. Why is it you want everyone to think you're a Mexican when you're not? In my family, everybody always wished they weren't. So she calls me names and means them because this really upsets her. Stupid, she calls me. Buttbreath. Say those in Spanish, I suggest to her, and we'll see what you know. She says, *Estúpido*. One wrong, I tell her. What about the other? No reply. You don't know, do you? Not a clue, right? This is a game we play, and though there is part of me that can't believe she takes it seriously, another part sees how my teasing bothers her too much.

"Besides, no Chicanos live in West Covina."

"Yes they do."

It cracks me up how serious she sounds. She's too easy. "I never met any from there, ever. It's probably too rich or something."

"You've never even been there, and I bet you don't even know where it is."

"Me and nobody like me."

"My parents just never taught me any Spanish."

"Did they talk it at home?"

"Not really."

"You see? What'd I tell you?"

"Asshole." She whispers that in my ear because we're on the floor and customers are around.

"When they were talking something, if they did, it probably was Italian and you didn't even know it."

I never tell my girlfriend Diana anything about these other girls. Though she's been mad at me anyway. We used to go out more often than we do now, but with my two jobs, and her school, it's almost only been weekends. After we go to a movie, we head back to her place because her parents go to sleep so early. I take her to the door and we kiss and then I leave. I park on the busy street around the corner and I walk back and crawl through her window. It's a big bedroom because she used to share with her sister, who went away to be a nurse. She's very sheltered in a certain way, in that Catholic way, but I'm not Diana's first boyfriend, though I am the first one she's made love to. She let me the second time we went out because she thought I expected it. Because I was so experienced. She's sixteen. She doesn't look it, but she acts it. She worries. She's scared of everything she likes. The first time she orgasmed, she told me a couple of months ago, she didn't really know what it was, and it felt too good, so she called her sister's best friend, who can talk about any subject and especially sex, and asked if she was all right.

She'll let me do certain things to her, and now she'll be on top sometimes. But she worries that one of us will get too loud. She has been a couple of times. I feel her pulsate in there real hard. She worries that we'll fall asleep after and her mom or dad will be up before we know it. That happened once, and I got out of there, but she's been really worried ever since about everything, every little noise, like they're listening.

The only thing in the room that isn't just for a girl is a statue I gave her of *The Thinker*. It came from Gifts. It had a chip in the wood base and was being sold at 20 percent discount. I kept looking at it, trying to decide if I should buy it. It's big, heavy. He looks smart. I imagined having it in my own place when I got one. I guess that Maria and Joan, the manager of our department, saw how often I stared at it, and so one day they gave it to me, all gift wrapped, a ribbon and bow. I was surprised, embarrassed even, that they bought me a present, and one so expensive, and I didn't think I should accept it, until they explained how it only cost a dollar — they'd marked it down as damaged and, being the manager and assistant manager, signed off on it. This was one of those nights that Diana came to the store to pick me up after work. She was suspicious of Maria, which seemed crazy to me since she was twenty-six and my boss, and then, as we were going down the escalator, of Cindy, who made a sexy wink at me, which didn't seem crazy. So right there in the parking lot I gave *The Thinker* to Diana, and it's been on her bedstand since.

"They got these pretty glass flowers," I say, "and I keep thinking of ways to get them for you. You know, cheap."

"They're not for me," she says. "Those are gifts for grandmothers or mothers."

"Well, then I could give them to your mom."

"A gift from you would be a good idea."

I'm not sure I want that yet. "I could give them to my mom, too. You know, for Mother's Day."

"You better not," she says. "It's stealing."

"Joan sells marked-down things all the time."

"I think you should stop thinking like this."

"But it's easy," I tell her. "I'm good at it."

"How do you know if you're good at it?"

"I know what I'm good at."

"You know I don't like that kind of talk."

"You *know* I don't *like* that kind of *talk*." Lately I've been imitating Maria de Covina.

"You better go," she says.

"Would you stop it," I say. "I'm playing, I'm only teasing."

"You really should go anyway," she says. She's naked, looking for her underwear in the bedsheets, in the dark. "I'm afraid. We're taking too many chances."

I don't take too many chances. One time I did sell something to a friend, for example, for a much lower price than was on the tag. But that was instead of, say, just giving it to him in the bag when he buys something else for a normal price. Which is stealing. I wouldn't do that. Another way is, a customer comes and buys an item, but instead of making a normal receipt, I ring it out on our long form, the one in three-colored triplicate, that one we use when the item has to be delivered. I wait for an expensive purchase. I give the customer the white copy, put the green copy in the register, then fill out the pink copy later — in blue pencil so it looks right, like it's from the stencil. I can stick whatever I want in a box, put that pink copy with a name and address on it, and mail it out of the store. The truth is I think of everything and do nothing. It's only a little game I play in my mind. There's nothing here I want. Well, one time I wanted a ship, a pirate ship to me, with masts and sails and rope the width of string. It was going off the floor because it never sold in over a year, and some items like this are smashed up and thrown away instead of sent back — written off as a loss. I thought I should just take it home instead of destroying it, but Maria insisted on writing me out a slip and selling it to me for three dollars. I gave it to my mom.

"If you really want the valise," I tell Mrs. Huffy, "I'll sell it to you marked down as damaged." Mrs. Huffy sells the luggage. She and I often work the same shift. Sometimes she comes over and sells gifts, and sometimes I sell luggage, but mostly we keep to our separate areas. Maria takes care of the silverware and china. The valise that Mrs. Huffy likes is going to be ripped up and trashed because it's not made anymore and can't be returned to the supplier for a refund.

"It seems like such a waste to throw it away." Mrs. Huffy fidgets with her glasses all the time. She has a chain on them so she doesn't put them down and forget them. You can't tell most of the time if she sees better with them off or with them on. Sometimes the glasses go nervously onto the top of her hair, which is silver gray, the same color as the chain and the frames.

"It is a waste if you ask me."

"You'd think they'd call the Salvation Army instead." Glasses hanging like a necklace.

Mrs. Huffy makes me think of what Diana will be like when she's old. Still worried. "But they're not. They're throwing it away."

"It's terrible," she says.

"I could just sell it to you."

She takes the glasses up to her nose and stares at me. "You can't do that. I wouldn't. Security looks at the receipt." When we leave the building at night, guards examine our belongings, and if we've bought anything from the store, they check the receipt to make sure it matches.

"We'll get it marked down. I'll ask Maria." Everything's okay if a manager or assistant manager says so.

"It wouldn't be right." Glasses on the head.

"Okay then, but I think it's no big deal."

"Do you think she'd do it?"

"I'm sure she would."

"I can't." Glasses on the nose. Holding the valise, snapping it open, snapping it closed. "I can't ask."

"I told you already I'd ask. I know she won't care."

"I don't know."

"*Como quieras*, whatever you decide." I'm walking back to Gifts because I see a customer.

"I don't know," Mrs. Huffy says. "Are you sure Maria would?"

Maria saw me the other night in the parking lot with Cindy, and she wouldn't stop asking me about it. So? she'd say, so? I didn't think I should talk about it. Come on, did you get some or not? I didn't think it was right to talk about it. But she kept insisting and, finally, it seemed okay. I told her how Cindy and I were parked near each other and she said something about a good-night kiss. She started pressing against me hard, and I just put my hand on a *chiche* and then she wrapped her leg around me even harder and rubbed up against me until she put her hand on me. She was physically hot, like sweating. She put her hand down there, I put my hand down there, and then we went into her car. I didn't want to tell Covina the rest, I didn't think I should. But still she says, So? Whadaya mean, *so?* I'm delaying because I feel her close behind me, and I'm not sure. Did you or not? she says. The store's just closed, and I'm at my register, clearing it while we're talking, about to take my tray out to count money, and she's behind me very close. Why don't you want to tell me? she says. She's got her *chiches* against me, moving just a little, and, I don't know, I don't mind but I'm embarrassed too. In case someone sees. But I don't say anything. I'm also surprised. I don't know why it hadn't crossed my mind. She had her register to clear, and she left.

"I don't like it." Diana's worrying. She's in pajamas.

"It's no big deal," I say. We're whispering to each other in the dark. I'm not sure why it's so dark this night but it is. I surprised her when I came to the window. I had to say her name a few times to wake her up.

"You better stop," she says. Even though I can't see them, the glass flowers I bought damaged are in a vase next to *The Thinker*. I told her I didn't want them for either her mom or mine, and once she saw them, how beautiful they were, she wanted them. "You're gonna get caught."

"You're gonna get *caught*," I say.

"Why would Maria be doing this?" she asks. "I don't trust her."

I feel like Diana is really sensing Cindy, or Liz. I told her I had to work Saturday night, and that's why we couldn't go out. I feel like it's because I'm talking too much about all this to Covina, and it's in the air, that I'm not being smart, talking *esas cosas* out loud. "Come on, it's crazy," I tell Diana. "She's a lot older than me, and she's the assistant manager of the department. She knows what she's doing."

Suddenly she starts crying.

"What's the matter?" I ask.

She's sobbing into her pillow.

"You're making too much noise," I'm whispering. "You're gonna wake up your parents."

"You have to go," she says. She's talking in a normal voice, which is really loud at this time of night. Her face is all wet. I try to kiss her, but she pushes me away. "You have to go," she says.

"Can't we make love?" I'm being quiet at the open window, and though my eyes have adjusted, it's so dark, and I can barely see her in the bed. "Don't you want to make love?"

I feel sick. I love women, but I realize I don't want to lose Diana. I love her.

Covina shakes her head as I tell her how Diana was acting. Mexican men, she says.

I do like it that she thinks of me as a man. I like being a man, even if it makes me feel too old for Diana. It's confusing. I'm not sure what to do. I wonder if she'd say the same if she didn't think I was almost twenty-one.

I go to the stockroom, and I sit on the edge of the gray desk. "Mrs. Huffy wants this valise real bad. You think you could sign this?" I've already made out a receipt. Instead of forty-five dollars, I made it for forty-five cents, damaged.

Covina gets up, and without kissing me, *ni nada,* she pushes her breast into my face. She has one hand under it, and another on my neck. Pretty quick she opens her blouse and she pulls up her bra and we're both excited and she reaches over and slams the stockroom door and she gets on her knees between mine. I wouldn't tell her, but nobody's ever done that to me before. It was exciting, and I was scared—it *was* right there in our stockroom—and I guess I am a little shocked too, but I don't want her to know it. You know. I follow her to her apartment because she told me to. Before I didn't even think about whether she had her own apartment. I didn't really want to go. And I didn't do very well. She probably saw how inexperienced I am really, and then I made the mistake of telling her how I'm in love with Diana, and how bad I'm feeling.

So I'm tired when I clock in because I stayed with her. I was late in the morning getting to A-Tron, and I wouldn't have gone in if I already didn't know there were a lot of orders we had to fill. Mrs. Huffy is already in Silverware and China when I get to the floor, so worried she can't even take her glasses off when she sees me, and Joan stops me in the middle of Gifts. Joan never works at night.

When Mrs. Huffy checked out with the valise, a security guard opened her package, and asked for the receipt, and the guard said he was going to keep it and make sure it was on the up and up the next day. Instead of, like, scratching the valise when she got home so it really did look damaged, instead of waiting for Joan to deal with it so she could tell us to never do anything like this again, Mrs. Huffy panicked and brought the valise back in the morning.

"Ms. Mata told me everything," Stemp says. Stemp works for the LAPD, or used to, or something like that. I already know who he is, but I'd never talked to him before. He never talks to anybody. He might be chief of security at The Broadway. He wears cheap black slacks and a cheap white shirt and a cheap, plain blue tie. He looks like he might rock in his swivel chair, but he doesn't. He just has it tilted back, his hands folded onto his *panza*. The office has no decorations, no photos or paintings or mirrors on the walls. On his gray desk is the cheapest lamp they sell in Furniture, which is across from Gifts, and one of those heavy black phones. He has a sheet of paper and a pen in front of him. "She told me about how you used triplicate forms and used our courtesy mailing service and how you sold goods to your friends." He stares at me for a very long time, satisfied like he just ate a big meal.

"I never did anything like that," I say. I couldn't believe Maria told him my ideas. "It's not true," I say.

"It's not true," he repeats. He shakes his head with only his eyes. "Do you realize that Ms. Mata was building a career here?"

"She didn't do anything. I know she never did anything."

He really shakes his head. "I don't have time for this. I already have it all." He slides the paper over to me. "Just sign it and get outta here."

I read his form. It lists all these ways I took things from the store, and how Maria cooperated.

"No," I say. "Maria didn't cooperate, she didn't do anything. I didn't do anything either."

"I can call the police right now if you'd prefer. We can deal with this in that manner."

"I guess. I have to think."

He sends me off after I sign a form admitting that I sold a forty-five-dollar valise to Mrs. Huffy for forty-five cents. I loved this job so much. I really loved being here at The Broadway, and I can't think of what I'll do now. I head to the parking lot, and I'm in my car, and I'm trying to decide whether I should go over to Diana's or to Maria's, if either of them would want to see me, when I see Liz waving at me. I get out of the car. How come you haven't called me? she wants to know. I'm wearing the suit I bought from her store. The vest is buttoned but the jacket isn't. I do always feel good in it.

Mayela One Day in 1989

I'm in a city called El Paso. I could point it out on a map. Right here, here it is. There is longitude, latitude. For most this is enough, a satisfactory explanation. But say we don't use all these imaginary concepts. Say there is no west of or east of or north of or south of. Forget all that. Forget these legalistic boundaries. No Texas here, no Mexico there, no New Mexico. Forget all that. Here's a river. Here are mountains. A sky above. Night, day. Sun and moon. Where there are people, there are buildings, and streets, and walkways. There are colorful and not so signs with messages that can be reduced to words. Eat. Sleep. Money. Work. Play. Away from those, and away from the buildings and people, the brown soil is a rock even at its surface. The vegetation is sparse, gray green, low to the ground, defensive. There is little water away from that river.

I walk on the streets. Or drive. Think about what I did before. How maps worked. I would open them and trace a road and I'd get there and I'd think I had discovered something, that I knew where I was. I'd go into a bar. Sit on a stool facing mirrors reflecting mirrors and bottles and think how this offered not just solace but solution. Or drugs. Or love. Or sex. I remember when I'd meet a woman. The old answer, the first answer. Find a woman, lose myself through a woman, find myself: Here I am.

Only a thick pane of glass and a sidewalk away, she's been glancing back at me—isn't she?—as she talks to a gray-haired man with a luxury car. She's huskier than him, a few inches taller, and as dramatic and endowed as fantasy: It's her red dress and wavy black hair and a blue, cloudless sky, as Mexican as cheap paint, that halos her, and a nasty kink in her eyes, which I can see even at this distance.

She is sitting across the booth I'm in. Her name is Mayela. We are in a coffee shop downtown where sunburned truck drivers talk the loudest in drawling English, tattoos on their hairy arms, wearing cowboy hats. Women, having lunch, wear nylons and high heels and imitation pearl necklaces. The coffee is too hot, too old, too black, too thin, and I color it with the white liquid that isn't milk. The waitress has a bun of hair bobby-pinned to the top of her head, two cloth flowers stitched into the net containing the bun. The mix is fertile and intoxicating, though like a drug cut with strychnine, there is an edge on the rush, a rustling breeze of death, and the whirl makes bold the blood and breath and muscle. When it has become later, the same restaurant, the sky blue red, too bright and gaudy to be anywhere else but here, there is no one else, not even the waitress pouring more coffee, and now she, not us, is the phantasm.

Mayela tells stories of men: fathers, brothers, cousins, lovers. Mayela has a husband. He lives in Houston, a dangerous American town where he left her by herself too often. She could not be alone like that, she says, as if of no more or less importance, and she never loved him. She only wanted to get away any way she could. Hers wasn't a home, that mud building near Chihuahua. It was her grandfather's house, and she slaved there, cleaning this, raking that, cooking, washing, nursing a grandmother and younger, fatherless children that were brother or half sister or cousin or niece and, then, also her

20

mother. Her mother stopped being well for so long that one day, Mayela says, she couldn't be sure if she was awake or asleep. So she married, at sixteen, and she had two children, and now she is here because she never loved that man. She cannot find a lover who can satisfy her. She is tormented by lovers. One, at twenty-two, is younger than her. Another, her boyfriend, is thirty-five, and he sometimes wants too much from her—he throws things and she doesn't know about him, and so she won't see him for days and sometimes weeks. The man with gray hair, almost sixty, treats her with elegance and dances with her in the middle of the day where lights are under the floor and tells her how to be near her is all he might ever ask for. He gave her a car, a used sports car. He says she can have a house that will be hers and he will carry the note. Mayela says she took the car but will pay for it and that she won't take the house. Because there's always payments.

I tell her how I feel sorry for her because a woman like her cannot live simply. She is monitored, never ignored. She is supposed to be more strong and more resistant than a man. Men always approaching her, making conversation supposed to not be about what it is. So many men, so much temptation. Too many temptations. Leaning toward her, making my voice as close as I want my body, I whisper *this*, *us*, that even as these words leave my lips, as my hands would move over her body, it is not me at all but *her*, that I am the one drawn in, that I will be the one caught and that she will be the one who has led me here. You, I tell Mayela, are temptress, and I am prey.

After we've sat for a while at a bar, after several mixed drinks, she suggests where we go next. It doesn't matter to me because I am with her and there is no better or worse.

21

We drive past the lights and the well-known streets. Past the old courthouse and the new jail into the dark, oldest part of town, where frail tenements are without plumbing or electricity, where the Spanish language is spoken in its most idiomatic form, so close to roots of meaning and sound that words breed like simple cells. Dark, so dark that stars glare like streetlights, while the moon hovers as in wilderness. Through this sludge of night we cross dead, metal ribs of train tracks, warehouses whose signs are brushed over chipping plaster and brick as frequently as gang tags. We glimpse bars whose decor and patrons, like the jukebox boasts and cries of love and death seeming to push open their doors, are as elemental as horses and goats and snakes, as leather and lard, as sweat and sunburn and rocks. We search these dark night streets with the simplest of names—First, Second, Third—because Mayela has forgotten, until we are there. Right there, look, where so many cars are innocently parked. At a corner. A yellow light over the door. Its name is above that light and can't be read easily: the Old Dominion.

I am with Mayela, and she has brought me here, and I hold her hand, and she grips mine in return. It is hot outside, hotter inside, and the music is full of rhythmic bass and pulsates like a drug against the glassy eyes of the men, so many men. No, they are not exactly the eyes of men and they are not exactly the eyes of women. One walks by in pants that are more a dress and a puffy shirt that is more a blouse and has long, straightened black hair but also a full-faced, trimmed beard. The rest are not so metaphorical. This is not a club to show off clothes or styles, not for satin or silk or suede, not animal-skin boots or brimmed hats. Only essences of style, what can survive in this desert, in the deepest west of all, where few things, or people, prosper.

I am holding Mayela's hand as she leads me past all of them for a space to stop and lean. Flesh is the steam of the club, the expiring hot moisture. Flesh. It's what I'm here for. There is no difference between them and me in this. Mayela stops and I remain very close to her.

These men want men in the Old Dominion and don't pretend indifference, don't disguise. And some women who want women too, and before several pass us they slow down, then from toe to head and mostly in between imagine Mayela. Mayela offers no reward for their attentions. They look at me and wink, raise eyebrows, hand-signal approval and envy. We are the most obvious here. Mayela is a large, tall woman, and full, and I stand over her in cowboy boots.

Mayela says something I don't hear over the pounding amps. The club is too crowded, and it is dirty, the brown, ever-blowing desert on the rug, bar, dance floor, even the moistened air is a dusty fog. A man approaches Mayela. They hug then talk into each other's ears, and she indicates for me to guard the drink I've bought her, and goes with him to the smooth floor in front of us. She dances without excess, with contented movements. The man twirls and spins around her, laughing, gesticulating, his hips and arms seductive, suggestive, very close to her body. Mayela's modest grin is constant and cooperative. I am drinking too much and it too disorients me. I order another for myself. I am remembering where I am. I am with Mayela, who is dancing with another man.

There are metal poles at the corners of the dance floor. They are bolted at the floor and ceiling. A few feet up, a crude platform circles each, and a muscular male dancer in a G-string undulates against his pole, rolling against and around it, riding, humping. It is a strain, frightening, because I don't want to see everything, and I fear the scoring on my psyche. Beneath the G-string are men, not women, men who are running their hands up and down the platform dancer, squeezing, caressing his calves and thighs and ass as he slides and rubs the pole between his legs, eyes closed in rapture. It is like my sexual yearning, only played out by a naked man against a pole with other men running their hands over him. Then again, no: When I want a woman, I want that one woman and not any woman, not Woman.

And Mayela is still dancing, though the man has left her. Now she is with a woman, and they are the only women on the dance floor, and the men are watching the two of them, and now I am watching them watch. In this heat they are sweating, their skin a milky pallor, thick and sticky.

I'm rubbing Mayela's neck while she listens to the woman she danced with. I want to feel her body, and I want to leave. I'm shaken, I'm drunk. She reaches around, touches my hand, but she has to listen to what I cannot hear. So I finish another drink.

Then we are on the dance floor, at the center, because Mayela has insisted on taking it. We are the spectacle, we are the couple. At the perimeters are the men, and those few women, seeing us, detailing. Mayela is circling me, her dress, yellow as sunshine, at once whirling away and clinging to her body. Hers is not a show for me, and not a show for them. It is for herself, as unconscious as trance. I'm miserable until I realize it is only the phantasm, and I am free. I am with Mayela. I am the man with Mayela.

Todd, it is explained, is a friend of Mayela's friend, the man she'd danced with. He is young, maybe twenty-one, and he knows Mayela from before. Todd, which is his favorite name, has bleached blond hair that is cut stylishly short. It is moussed, he tells us. Todd has drawn the faintest of purple lines around his black Mexican eyes. We are outside the club, leaning against parked cars, smoking marijuana. It's late. It is still dark, the only light the dim one above the club entrance facing the other street. Power lines drape over us, linked from one wooden pole to another, hanging above buildings, going in here and there, never visibly ending. Swamp coolers stand on top of the roofs, waiting for daylight. It is dark except for the hot cherry of the joint and Mayela's yellow dress and Todd's white shirt buttoned to the top, and stars that remind us the desert is beneath and around us, and the moon, and the red square taillights becoming smaller on the street's horizon until they are no more.

Todd has been cruising several guys this evening. He doesn't know which will work out for him. He has split with Mayela's friend. She understands about him, he tells her.

He talks with a need to, and Mayela and I must listen to him. Mayela asks about his brother. He has tested positive, Todd says, but he doesn't have it yet, it is still dormant. He takes pills he gets in Juárez, Todd says. It is quiet and so hot, even with a breeze. His brother still likes to dress up, Todd says. He puts on a dress and goes out. He wants to have the operation but how, and, with this disease possibility, he is in a panic. He is so scared and lost and confused, Todd explains. It is quiet except when someone else enters or exits the club and the music pours out, jackhammering the sidewalk and asphalt. And then suddenly Todd changes his mood and pitch. His brother's such a whore, and he wants to live as much as he can *now!* And then, as abruptly, Todd drops this subject and begins to talk about himself and the man he is most interested in tonight.

Stop. I have to leave. We have to go.

I'm not sure where I'm driving but we are back in the lights of downtown, away from the stars. I'm telling Mayela that it was, it was, that I was trying. She says she's used to it. And she likes these men. They are a challenge to her, she says.

A challenge? The car windows are down, and the wind, like the heat, is an unmistakable presence.

For example, she says, her friend. Who is Todd's friend. She knows he wanted her. Tonight when she was dancing, the woman, she knew that woman wanted her. But so did he. Did I notice? She says she always knows these women want her, but her satisfaction comes from knowing she has attracted a man like Todd's friend, because he doesn't want women. Only a special woman. She *knew*, she tells me brightly, proud, that he wanted her. Did I understand how she knew?

I see the dancer in the G-string riding that pole.

Mayela's face is the color of a kiln-dried, earthen mask. Her nose is broad, her cheeks are high, her eyes slant and are as secret as love and fear. Mayela is not only beautiful. Only I don't know the mythology, I don't know the gods or the demons.

I am alert and I remember where I am going: to the bar where she parked the sports car her gray-haired man gave her.

You think I'm a lesbian? she asks, noticing my shift.

I'm imagining Todd's brother in a dress. Or I'm imagining her riding the metal pole between her legs. I can't think of what to say though, so I don't say anything. And I'm not sure about what she is asking me.

Well I'm not, she tells me. She too distances, seems confused.

I stop in the parking lot next to her sports car. I turn my head toward her, and say, This is when it's supposed to be the good-night kiss, isn't it?

We don't *kiss* good night, she informs me, both mad and hurt.

We. I see Todd's friend rubbing himself against her on the dance floor.

Good night.

Slowly she opens the door for herself. Slowly she walks to her own car. I wait, politely, for her to get inside, to start the motor.

I am in El Paso. It is 1989.

Hueco

Mrs. Hargraves's tongue was blood-red with deep blue veins on its underside. I knew because she was smiling, and lots of those teeth in front weren't there, and her tongue licked the top gaps. "It's directly upstairs," she said, so happy about her success in placing a newspaper ad. "It's the biggest apartment I rent. You're going to like it. I don't have a doubt, because everyone does." Her teeth, the few still wobbling, mostly bottoms, weren't too pretty either.

She disappeared into another room. I waited at the threshold of the double glass doors that opened to what was either a dining or living room, maybe both, I couldn't be sure, entranced by two beautifully hand-carved Mexican chiffoniers, which were draped by an assortment of browning doilies, round and oval and square, lapping over one another, on which were a collection of ceramic farm animals, almost every one chipped, or missing a wing, or an ear, or a tail, and even a lot of the head in a couple of instances. Looming huge on the wall over them was a darkened oil painting of a wild turkey about to fly.

But it was a blue carpet that cast the spell over the room. The bluest carpet I'd ever seen. The first and only blue carpet I'd ever seen. It was shag, the long-strand kind that gets matted and tangled in many directions and finally goes stiff and flat. It was real dirty, and it'd been there too long getting even dirtier. It probably couldn't be vacuumed was probably why it wasn't.

"It's right up the stairs," Mrs. Hargraves said once she got back. She quit moving and whipped her tongue straight in my face again. "Up those stairs right behind you."

I was blocking her way out. I'd gotten disoriented and almost seemed to forget what I came for. I backed up, and she passed by me. She wore a long, navy blue dress with white flowers all over it. Petunias? This rug, a wall-to-wall, also continued with us up the stairs.

"Right here's the bathtub and sink and toilet." A door, the first on the right at the top of the stairs, was open. We took a couple of more steps and Mrs. Hargraves, stopping in front of the next door, pointed at the two closed ones around a corner hallway. "The far apartment is where Mr. De la O lives." Her voice trembled just a touch. She was comfortable with it. To me it was part of her accent. "He's an invalid and I take care of him. The other is Mr. Omann's."

"That's funny," I said.

Mrs. Hargraves didn't follow.

"You know, their names. De la *O* and *O*mann." I emphasized the O's when I said the names for clarity. "They're uncommon. And both have those O's."

Mrs. Hargraves, unsmiling, her veined tongue not exposed, considered my comments deep behind her blue eyes before she would open the door. I realized something else as her tongue reamed her cheeks. That the hall was a chalky baby blue. All of it. The ceiling, the crown molding at the top, the wood trim in the middle of the wall, the base trim, all of it was painted with the same flat, unglossy, dusty paint.

My powder-blue apartment door opened to the powder-blue kitchen. The floor was white linoleum with bluebonnets, which of course are blue. The little table in the center was chromed metal, imitation wood, brown, with four padded chairs. A modernistic design in blue vinyl.

Through the kitchen was a fully furnished bedroom. "My mother passed in this room," Mrs. Hargraves told me. "On that bed."

"I'm sorry," I said.

She appreciated my sympathy. "It was a number of years ago. My grandmother did her passing on here as well. I cared for my bedridden mother for so many years in this room. It was after that I divided the house for renters."

There was an upholstered couch and matching chair and a wooden one and a couple of lamps in the big living room area through the bedroom door.

"I'll take it," I said. "This is lots more than I could've hoped for."

"Didn't I just tell you?" she said satisfied. "Everybody loves this apartment."

"Can I move in today?"

"Now what is it you do, Fernando?"

"Fernandez is my last name," I told her again. "I'm a carpenter."

"A carpenter! It'll be so good to have a carpenter here!" Mrs. Hargraves was smiling unbashfully again, showing off the shadowy gaps and that tongue's lean muscularity.

I wasn't a carpenter. I'd changed tires for a while there. Fixed all the flats. Then I'd been a painter. Meaning I painted with a roller, on a crew. Then I helped some electricians. My longest job was working with brick masons, shoveling cement into the mixer and out to a wheelbarrow and hefting cinder blocks off flatbed trucks and restacking them. I especially hated that work, even though it lasted a long time. Really I was a laborer. That was my title. I was working around carpenters often though, and I admired them. It was a job I believed I wanted someday if nothing else came up. A skill to be proud of, that paid well. Really I swept up, got tools and cords and material for carpenters as well as others. I was working at a remodeling project downtown. One of the guys I didn't like called me grunt. As in, Hey, grunt.

I chose to think more highly of myself. Embrace my strengths and abilities and have goals. I wasn't going to allow mess-ups, or whatever you'd call them, anymore.

I had two loves, Yvette and Blanca. I met Yvette at a bar. She was my real girlfriend, the one I saw. I met Blanca at a bar too, weeks after I met her at Walgreen's when I bought a wide-ruled spiral notebook. She was with the girlfriend of a welder I'd worked with at another job, and he'd told me where she liked to hang out. She told me her boyfriend was a hairstylist. A beautician? I asked her. What kind of man would be a beautician? I decided it couldn't be very serious. That I had a chance with her. She was the one I desired. I'd marry Blanca. I wanted to write poetry for her. In Spanish, the language of love. Or letters. *Mi querida Blanca, mi amor, mi vida. Sin ti, ¿qué vida? Si no con los brazos y las manos, si no con besos, pues, con los sentimientos de amor y sueño.* She was the only woman I'd ever want, ever. I could barely think of her without longing. She was sex and love. She was woman. She was breasts and hips and lips. She was kissing. She was babies. I would be so good with Blanca, but I didn't have an idea of how to prove it to her. I'd never had much luck, and it seemed like I was on a bad run of it. It had to be her. If it were her, God, please, everything, every single one of them, would be good from then on.

Yvette was more than all right. I'm not complaining, and I'm not criticizing her. She was who she was and proud of it. She was the kind that might have been a *chola* if that's how it worked out. Or a biker's old lady. She was working at Tony Lama boots, stitching. Strong hands. For such a small woman she was big, as in muscular, though she was soft in her big heart, and could laugh big too. Bad, a little wild, not afraid of anybody. Not afraid to go after what she wanted. A big voice, big confidence. Big in fun places too. We liked drinking rum and Cokes in Juárez on Friday night. She'd grown up only a few streets north of Mrs. Hargraves's and didn't understand what I could praise about this old house and dirty neighborhood so I told her. How it had been a mansion really, back when Montana Street was the highest-class boulevard in town at the turn of the century, when people cruised in the horse and carriage. Rich people. Rich white people. And none of these Mrs. Hargraves–type ladies either. I didn't think so anyway. All she had to do was consider how much house this was if the upstairs had a sitting room — I called it — which, I guessed, went on to the other side of the wall too, into the apartment there. Once I got used to living here, which was after about ten days, after finally letting my mind wander, I explained how I had a few insights. How the blue was about something and not just cheap paint, or not only so. There was some kind of meaning. No, I didn't know what, I wasn't saying I knew that. I could show her all the different blues. Besides the obvious, like the couch and stuffed chair, I pointed out the skies and lakes in the two paintings on the wall. Where the paper flowers were easy to see, I showed her the slightest hint of blue stain in the cut-glass vase that held them, which you could see if you looked through a white light bulb. Anything in the room that could be painted that pale blue, was. "*Watcha*," I said, "even the lamp shades." For some reason, the paint there was hardest to notice until you did. Then it was the most conspicuous. I ran my finger down the one near us. "See how it comes off?" I smeared the dry powder across her soft cheek. I turned the lamp off, letting the light in the kitchen illuminate what was necessary.

Yvette giggled like she was six and ticklish under her arms and around her waist, until little tears dribbled at the corners of her eyes. That was when I noticed her eyeshadow was blue too. I couldn't tell her though.

We were making out on the lumpy blue couch when we heard Mr. De la O on the toilet. Or was it Mr. Omann? It was on the other side of a thin Sheetrock wall, hidden from view but not ten feet from where we embraced. It was not a wall from the original house. It was at this particular moment that I realized a Mr. O sat there much of the night the other evenings as well. I hadn't registered the importance of him or the toilet until right then, with Yvette's body next to me warm.

I shook my head, embarrassed. He was groaning, straining, though not too loud, burning a cigarette with, I imagined, his pants below his knees.

"That must be Mr. De la O," I told Yvette quietly. "I think he has some troubles with the digestion, or, how would you say, the thing that goes after." He was making even more guttural sounds now. "Mr. De la Ugggh," I whispered.

Yvette really lost it and started laughing hysterically. I told her how discourteous and disrespectful she was being, how she might cause more problems for the older gentleman if she made him self-conscious. I suggested we move to the bedroom.

We landed in the *hueco*—that's what I called it—of the old double bed. It was the side anybody would have naturally slept on. I slept there because it was unavoidable. I'd tried to avoid it when I first moved in. You know, because of Mrs. Hargraves's mother, and her grandmother. At first I imagined that this mattress indentation was where their dead bodies were found. At the deepest basin of the hollow it was inches lower than the rest of the old mattress. What their dying or even dead bodies created. At first I didn't even pull back the blue bedspread. I didn't want to find anything. Like gray hairs. I got used to it though. Now Yvette and I were in it with our clothes off because that was inevitable too, the most natural place for our bodies to go. Even though the *hueco* wasn't exactly in the middle of the mattress. It was just a little off center. Close to a nightstand, away from the blue wall.

When Yvette made her pleasure noises, when I wanted to make some of my own, I kept thinking of my neighbors' names. I really had forgotten which one lived behind which door.

They said it was a strain of flu unheard of in the history of El Paso. From China, or from Russia, or from Malaysia. From somewhere so far away. Very far away. Some wet place unknown and not so good for us who lived near Mexico and in the desert. Not like us at all. I crossed that border. Feverish, hallucinatory dreams. I could never see them. I was having them and I could never see them. Like they didn't exist if I did. That kind of fever and sweat. And in it, Mrs. Hargraves was standing above me, at the foot of the bed. Fernando, she said. She disapproved of me being ill. She disapproved of me. Rent money? I gave it to her, or I told her where to find it. Or I apologized. I was sick, so I wasn't too clear. She stood above me. Blue eyes. The blue veins in her tongue. I was on my back in the *hueco*. That hollow her mother shaped. Or followed after her mother. Years to form. Years in the room, on the mattress. Waiting. Looking up, sick, delirious. Seeing this Mrs. Hargraves. Who never stared down at a lasting creation. Her mother and grandmother were all I knew of her life. That she stood above these dying bodies, over them. Disapproving? Her mother might have been dead for days. In the hole where I was sweating, hot. Once I got up for water and I returned shivering and pulled the covers over me. And then I traveled with the fever, far away, where there was no memory, no history.

A note from Mrs. Hargraves:

> Fernando: Don't be so lazy
> empty your garbage & wash your
> dishes. I am not empty any
> more garbage. You no you
> don't get maid service hear.
> You never have moped your
> kitchen or vacum. I never had
> a renter so dirty. I can not
> take care of you. I will tell
> you in person Saturday.
> Hargraves.

I'd been writing in the notebook I bought at Walgreen's about Blanca. I loved Blanca so stupidly. When I made love with Yvette, I wished for Blanca. I wanted only Blanca. Blanca Blanca. I would write poetry in the notebook. Blanca was in school, going to the community college to become a medical secretary. I wanted to go to college too. I would study blueprints and have my own business someday. Blueprints. I wrote Blanca letters that I never sent. I really wished I knew if I were writing poetry. I thought some of it was. Someday, when she saw the lines, she'd think they were. She'd be so shocked when she learned I had written verses about her. Proud if we were together. Surprised that I had and disappointed in herself if she wasn't with me yet. Blanca was salvation. I prayed to God and to the mother of God. Please God. Please. *Por favor, Madre de Dios, Virgencita.*

My note to Mrs. Hargraves:

Stay out of this
apartment. As long as I am
renting this apartment you
have NO right to enter unless
I approve or you ask in
advance.

I have done NO damage to
this apartment. I only have 2
forks, 2 spoons, 1 knife, 2
plates, 3 glasses. How could
I make a mess with so little?
I never cook. How I keep my
dishes or how much trash I
have in the grocery sack is MY
business and is NOT your
business. It is MY business.

I DID NOT ask you to be a
"maid" for me. YOU decided to
be the "maid." I do not want
your services. I let you come
in this apartment because I
thought it was a trade: you
come in but you wash the
dishes.

At least when I wash the
dishes I use HOT water and
SOAP and put them away CLEAN.
It is disgusting to find
grease and dried lumps on my 2
plates and my utensils.

I would be happy to
discuss this with you
Saturday.
R. Fernandez

I went to the bar to see if I'd see her again. Except for Friday
I went every night until she came in with that welder's girlfriend.
Ex now. When she told me she wasn't dating the hairstylist, I
asked her out. I was so excited and encouraged. My pure prayers
would be answered. She was in white. A tight, short white dress,
her full body pushing on it everywhere. Her long black hair and
eyes and high-heeled shoes. Her legs were dark smooth skin,
no nylons. I would never have believed Blanca could say no like
that. *Jamás.* Never. Her word. She mocked me. Was I crazy,
she said. It was not a question. Was I crazy. She laughed. She
was serious too. I had no doubt. I wasn't close. She had never,
never thought of me. The one she still loved was a hairstylist.
She wanted to get back with him. She loved him, yes. She didn't
want to know me better. No, she didn't even remember me, she
didn't remember last time or Walgreen's. Oh yes, him. No.
Never. Was I crazy.

This was difficult for me to accept. I'd only fallen in love, real
love, this once. I couldn't explain it. Not to myself, not to her. I
loved her for all her specifics, even though I only imagined them,
didn't even know her, never knew her.

I washed my utensils in very hot water. The truth was that I
didn't have any dish detergent. I kept forgetting to buy some.
But the water got very hot. The two forks, the two spoons. Only
one plate but all the glasses. Suddenly I didn't want to be a carpenter anymore either. I didn't want any of those trades. I was
trying to think of another occupation. Though not a hairstylist.
I didn't believe Blanca. Not really. She was upset, confused. It
must be hard to be so much woman, to make decisions about

love. I'd figure her out. She made me upset too. I opened my Walgreen's notebook. Stared at the blue lines. I saw Blanca with no clothes on. Her breasts. Her stomach and small waist, the wide hips around her pubic area. It was like a girlie magazine. On Friday night Yvette made her pleasure noises under me and over me. Now for fun she called them Mr. Omann, Mr. De la O. And she laughed loud, so happy. We held each other in the *hueco* of the mattress. We made ourselves fit, like we were in a shallow bathtub together, looking over the edges.

"What does it feel like to you?" I asked her. I ran a finger below her eyebrows, on the pasty blue eyeshadow.

"I like it," she said. "I like everything."

"Really?" I asked. I had my right hand on her big breast, a finger on her dark nipple. I was smearing some of the blue eyeshadow on it. I liked her fine. I only imagined she was Blanca sometimes. Yes, I loved Blanca. Ached for her. It wasn't fair. Blanca was too beautiful. Yvette was cute though, and fun, and I really liked that she liked me. She didn't know anything about Blanca though, and I couldn't hurt her feelings. I wouldn't either. I knew I was a lucky guy to have her. She liked me touching her breasts. All her body, but she really liked me touching her breasts the most.

"Do you like blue?" I asked.

"Blue what?" she said.

"Blue. You know, blue."

"Blue," she said. "I like yellow. What if everything was yellow?" She laughed, and her breast moved under my hand.

We heard the pounding up the blue-shag-rug-padded stairs afterward. We remembered hearing the sound. We remembered hearing the blue door of my apartment being opened afterward too. Standing above us, at the foot of the *hueco*, where her mother died, where her grandmother died, Mrs. Hargraves made a silent O. She showed her teeth and the places there were no teeth and her tongue. Yvette had her legs wrapped around me and I was inside her. We saw her and we both heard, right then, not afterward, a loud O coming from her mouth.

A note from Mrs. Hargraves:

> For Mr. Fernando — I am
> surprise and disgusted by you.
> I have *sick folk* or I would
> answered first note first
> before I went and found you
> and that horror. Just
> understand this. (*You have
> my apt in my home*). not a apt
> house or Dog pound. I check
> on all my places like I did
> when I find you with that
> horror. so you go to hell.
> Move if you don't like me I
> would be happy. I have 2
> other men renters not only
> renters but friends so you go
> to hell understand. Thats my
> own families bed for many
> years that you were in bed
> with that horror. I will be
> hear saturday if possible. I
> do not want no women no
> horrors coming in I will not
> have it. So you move no more
> notes. I am boss hear not
> you. Hargraves.

Hueco

I was in the *hueco*, my eyes on the water stain in the blue ceiling above me. It had a whirling form that I could shape and reshape. My mind couldn't stop dreaming in it now. Was it only a flu? That sickness came, then left. Twenty-four hours, maybe thirty-six. I'd missed a day of work. I'd taken a Sunday walk over to Juárez but I didn't eat anything there. I walked over the Santa Fe Bridge, walked to the cathedral, crossed myself in front of San Judas after I read the prayer, walked back. I didn't go there for Saint Jude, or to go to the cathedral. I had just ended up there. I hadn't gone to church in many years. I walked in because others were, because a priest was conducting a Mass. Though it was Sunday, there was no special meaning for me. I gave a beggar two pesos on the way back. She was curled up in the shade, all in black, her gray hair under a black scarf. I stepped over huge holes in the sidewalk. Passed through the border-guard station after only one question, kept walking. I walked a long walk. I never once felt sick or feverish. Until I got back. Then I started getting hot. I got in the bed. I was so hot I was cold and I shivered. The water stain was like television, and time was like memory, and the stain was spinning and twisting. And Mrs. Hargraves was coming in and disapproving of me. And the stain was moving inside me. And the stain was playing in my mind when I turned my face away, as my body sagged, limp, into the *hueco*.

My note to Mrs. Hargraves, written neatly on the wide-ruled paper, ripped as neatly as possible from the spiral notebook from Walgreen's. I thought it was a very well written letter. Maybe not the end. I was sorry about that:

Dear Mrs. Hargraves,
      I was taught to respect
      my elders. Perhaps there are
      exceptions, especially when
      they insult me.

I did not care too much
about your coming in at first,
though you have no legal right
to enter this apartment, which
you have rented to me. You
ask a lawyer if you do not
believe me. I have never had
a landlady enter an apartment
I have rented and dump my
trash and wash my dishes and
then complain about it. This
place was filthy when I moved
in and will be no more filthy
when I decide to move out.

I thought you were a nice
lady when I moved in. When I
asked you to please not come
in I thought you were able to
understand.

I have been thinking
about how the door will look
when I nail it closed every day
with sixteen penny nails.
They are the biggest nails.
They make very good locks. It
will be fun to drive them in
and pull them out every day.

I will have anybody, male
or female, come into my
apartment whenever I want. I
am sorry I am not queer. I
only like women though.

Hueco

I will not tell you to go
to hell like you did me, boss.
R. Fernandez

"But why a television?" I asked Yvette. She'd brought it over
and set it up at the foot of the bed. First she carried in one of
the chairs from the kitchen, then she put the TV there. It was a
Wednesday evening. She took her clothes off and we both fell
into the mattress *hueco* and when she made noises she moaned
the other tenants' names, satisfied and smiling. I was beginning
to get used to her.

"It's only a black and white," she said. "And the reception is
bad. Or the tube. I'm not sure. But it's all I got."

Shout

He beat on the screen door. "Will somebody open

this?!" Unlike most men, he didn't leave his hard hat in his truck, he took it inside his home, and he had it in his hand. His body was dry now, at least wasn't like it was two hours ago at work, when he wrung his T-shirt of sweat, made it drool between the fingers of his fist, he and his partner making as much of a joke out of it as they could. That's how hot it was, how humid, and it'd been like this, in the nineties and hundreds, for two weeks, and it'd been hot enough before that. All he could think about was unlacing his dirty boots, then peeling off those stinky socks, then the rest. He'd take a cold one into the shower. The second one. He'd down the first one right at the refrigerator. "Come on!" Three and four were to be appreciated, five was mellow, and six let him nap before bed.

"I didn't hear you," his wife said.

"Didn't *hear* me? How *couldn't* you hear me? And why's it locked anyways? When I get here I don't feel like waiting to come in. Why can't you leave the thing unlocked?"

"Why do you think?"

"Well don't let the baby open it. I want this door open when I get home." He carried on in Spanish, *hijos de* and *putas* and *madres* and *chingadas*. This was the only Spanish he used at home. He tossed the hard hat near the door, relieved to be

49

inside, even though it was probably hotter than outside, even though she was acting mad. He took it that she'd been that way all day already.

Their children, three boys, were seven, four, and almost two, and they were, as should be expected, battling over something. "Everybody shut up and be quiet!" he yelled. Of course that worsened the situation, because when he got mad he scared the baby, who immediately started crying.

"I'm so tired," he muttered.

She glared at him, the baby in her arms.

"You know sometimes I wish you were a man cuz I wouldn't let you get away with looks like that. I wouldn't take half the shit I take from you." He fell back into the wooden chair nobody sat in except him when he laced the high-top boots on, or off, as he already had. "You know how hot it was today? A hundred and five. It's unbelievable." He looked at her closely, deeply, which he didn't often do, especially this month. She was trying to settle down the baby and turned the TV on to distract the other two.

"It's too hard to breathe," he said to her. He walked bare-footed for the beer and took out two. They were in the door tray of the freezer and almost frozen.

"So nothing happened today?" she asked. Already she wasn't mad at him. It was how she was, why they could get along.

"Nothing else was said. Maybe nothing's gonna happen. God knows this heat's making everybody act unnatural. But tomorrow's check day. If he's gonna get me most likely it'll be tomorrow." He finished a beer leaning against the tile near the kitchen sink, enjoying a peace that had settled into the apartment. The baby was content, the TV was on, the Armenians living an arm's reach away were chattering steadily, there was a radio on from an apartment in a building across from them, Mexican TV upstairs, pigeons, a dog, traffic noise, the huge city out there groaning its sound—all this silence in the apartment.

"There's other jobs," he said. "All of 'em end no matter what anyways."

It was a job neither of them wanted to end too soon. This year he'd been laid up for months after he fell and messed up his shoulder and back. He'd been drunk—a happy one that started after work—but he did it right there at his own front door, playing around. At the same time the duplex apartment they'd been living in for years had been sold and they had to move here. It was all they could get, all they were offered, since so few landlords wanted three children, boys no less, at a monthly rent they could afford. They were lucky to find it and it wasn't bad as places went, but they didn't like it much. They felt like they were starting out again, and that did not seem right. They'd talked this over since they'd moved in until it degenerated into talk about separation. And otherwise, in other details, it also wasn't the best year of their lives.

He showered in warm water, gradually turning the hot water down until it came out as cold as the summer allowed, letting the iced beer do the rest.

She was struggling getting dinner together, the boys were loud and complaining about being hungry, and well into the fifth beer, as he sat near the bright color and ever-happy tingle of the TV set, his back stiffening up, he snapped.

"Everybody has to shut up! I can't stand this today! I gotta relax some!"

She came back at him screaming too. "I can't stand *you*!"

He leaped. "You don't talk to me like that!"

She came right up to him. "You gonna hit me?!" she dared him.

The seven-year-old ran to his bed but the other two froze up, waiting for the tension to ease enough before their tears squeezed out.

"Get away from me," he said trying to contain himself. "You better get away from me right now. You know, just go home, go to your mother's, just go."

"*You* go! *You* get out! We're gonna stay!"

He looked through her, then slapped a wall, rocking what seemed like the whole building. "You don't know how close you are."

He wouldn't leave. He walked into the bedroom, then walked out, sweating. He went into the empty kitchen—they were all in the children's room, where there was much crying—and he took a plate and filled it with what she'd made and went in front of the tube and he clicked on a ball game, told himself to calm himself and let it all pass at least tonight, at least while the weather was like it was and while these other things were still bothering both of them, and then he popped the sixth beer. He wasn't going to fall asleep on the couch tonight.

Eventually his family came out, one by one peeking around a corner to see what he looked like. Then they ate in a whisper, even cutting loose here and there with a little giggle or gripe. Eventually the sun did set, though that did nothing to wash off the glue of heat.

And eventually the older boys felt comfortable enough to complain about bedtime. Only the baby cried—he was tired and wanted to sleep but couldn't because a cold had clogged his nose. Still, they were all trying to maintain the truce when from outside, a new voice came in: SHUT THAT FUCKING KID UP YOU FUCKING PEOPLE! HEY! SHUT THAT FUCKING KID UP OVER THERE!

It was like an explosion except that he flew toward it. He shook the window screen with his voice. "You fuck yourself, asshole! You stupid asshole, you shut your mouth!" He ran out the other way, out the screen door and around and under the heated stars. "Come on out here, mouth! Come out and say that to my face!" He squinted at all the windows around him, no idea where it came from. "So come on! Say it right now!" There was no taker, and he turned away, his blood still bright red.

When he came back inside, the children had gone to bed and she was lying down with the baby, who'd fallen asleep. He went back to the chair. The game ended, she came out, half-closing the door behind her, and went straight to their bed. He followed. "I dunno," he said after some time. He'd been wearing shorts and nothing else since his shower, and it shouldn't have taken him so long, yet he just sat there on the bed. Finally he turned on the fan and it whirred, ticking as it pivoted left and right. "It doesn't do any good, but it's worse without it." He looked at her like he did earlier. "I'm kinda glad nobody came out. Afterwards I imagined some nut just shooting me, or a few guys coming. I'm getting too old for that shit."

She wasn't talking.

"So what did they say?" he asked her. "At the clinic?"

"Yes."

"Yes what?"

"That I am."

They both listened to the fan and to the mix of music from the Armenians and that TV upstairs.

"I would've never thought it could happen," he said. "That one time, and it wasn't even good."

"Maybe for you. I knew it then."

"You did?"

She rolled on her side.

"I'm sorry about all the yelling," he said.

"I was happy you went after that man. I always wanna do stuff like that."

He rolled to her.

"I'm too sticky. It's too hot."

"I have to. We do. It's been too long, and now it doesn't matter."

"It does matter," she said. "I love you."

"I'm sorry," he said, reaching over to touch her breast. "You know I'm sorry."

He took another shower afterward. A cold shower. His breath sputtered and noises hopped from his throat. He crawled into the bed naked, onto the sheet that seemed as hot as ever, and listened to outside, to that mournful Armenian music mixing with Spanish, and to the fan, and it had stilled him. It was joy, and it was so strange. She'd fallen asleep and so he resisted kissing her, telling her. He thought he should hold on to this as long as he could, until he heard the pitch of the freeway climb, telling him that dawn was near and it was almost time to go back to work.

The Pillows

While I was at the Albuquerque airport bar—
Pueblo turquoise and sandstone—waiting to meet my girlfriend,
a woman offered to buy me a drink. She was better than good-
looking. We each ordered a frozen margarita, did a *salud*, and I
walked her politely to her gate, and she kissed my lips as she
went to the plane at the very last minute—she had a first-class
seat. I came back to the bar and ordered both a shot and another margarita. In less than fifteen minutes my girlfriend's
plane was supposed to arrive. It was one of those days when I
was a man. My head was shaking when a starched white shirt
and tie, coat slung over the shoulder, came up to me.

"George," he said. His speech was timid and a little too for-
mal. It was always hard for me to figure out these guys who wore
business suits. "You don't remember me? From El Paso. Austin
High?"

It took me a few seconds to connect. "Ibáñez?"

I was right. I stood up and shook his hand harder than he
did mine. "How's it going, Daniel?" I said his first name with a
Spanish pronunciation, un-Americanized. I was conscious of
this immediately, and I was sure he remembered me as the guy
who didn't like it back in the old days when an Anglo coach or
teacher would say it their way, like they were right and the other
was wrong. I was still that same guy, even though my own legal

name was Jorge, like my father and his father. It's just that I didn't happen to like my name in Spanish. I thought George was better. And that was always my point anyway: Our choice, not theirs.

Danny and I went to Austin High School a hundred years ago, though we didn't hang out together. He was a better student than me, and that was probably why we never had any of the same classes. But we started elementary at the same time, at Crockett, and that was enough for us to know each other forever. It must've been around sixth or seventh that we separated off. We played on the same Little League team one season. He was left field, sometimes third base. I played short and pitched. He was fast, I was strong. We made the city play-offs that year.

"So you get back much?" I asked.

"I'm living there," he said.

"Really?" Everybody who grew up in El Paso hated it and left when they could, as soon as possible. There was nothing to do, and no jobs, let alone good-paying ones. If you were raised there, it seemed like any other city was better. You sensed this if you hadn't ever gotten away, and knew when you had. The best thing about El Paso was that people thought you were cool and tough for growing up there.

"It's what I'm doing here. Flying back."

"Really?" Leaving El Paso was for good. Moving back was almost unheard of. There were two possible explanations. You had no choice—desperate, tragic economics—or your parents, who of course were still there, were old, and somebody had to take care of them. That was cultural, and the best part of El Paso. "You actually have a job El Chuco? *Pues, ¿qué haces hay?*"

"I'm a newspaper editor."

"Like a reporter?"

"No. Though I used to be a reporter. I did that in Dallas, then in L.A. I took the job in El Paso as the paper's editor." He looked at me carefully, like he was wondering if I was aware how much his suit was worth. "I was the first Hispanic to have it."

"First Hispanic, huh?"

He caught my sound like he did when I pronounced his name. It's an ancient discussion made new again—who we are, where we're from. Like saying you were "Spanish," how they called us years ago, this one implied the light-skinned Iberian Peninsula too. No one I ever knew in El Paso, Tejas, dark or *güero*, had a single relative from *pinche* Spain. These words were a way to avoid saying you had Mexican descent, that Mexico was too low-class. Even if it was out of public fashion, I felt like I was the last one to still say I was a Chicano. Maybe it was a dead issue left over from the old days, but not to me.

"Congratulations," I told him, letting it loose. "That *is* great. I bet El Paso's up to like ninety percent of us Mexicans by now. *Que duro*, that town. Yeah, it's about fucking time they noticed us living there. That's great. You gotta be proud. You should be."

I'd made him happy.

"I can't imagine the newspaper having stories about people from the neighborhood," I went on. "Did they ever?"

"It was bad. Gangs and graffiti stories. Sometimes about how to make tamales."

Even as he told me this he was somber, too dry. "So you're kicking ass. That's great, Daniel."

"I did all right." He paused and looked off.

"Really," I said. The pause was loud. I told him about my art.

"What're you doing here?" he asked.

"*Mi locura*," I said. "I'm broke, but I got a girlfriend . . ."

"I saw her," he said.

"You saw her?"

"Yeah, you lucky bastard."

"You mean that woman at this bar?"

"Couldn't miss her."

"She ain't her, man. My baby hasn't gotten off the plane yet."
He laughed. "And I can't find one."

"She's coming in from Denver, and I'm waiting here for her
plane."

"And this other, you just met her?"

"She lives in New York City and says she was out here for a
shoot. Do you believe it? Says she's a model. Sat right up next
to me and started talking and shit."

"What a lucky bastard. If I were you I'd go out and buy a
stack of lottery tickets immediately. You may never be so hot
again as long as you live."

"*Sabes qué,* Daniel, *tienes razón,* that's smart business advice."

Smiling, we're both shaking our heads now. My girlfriend's
747 was gleaming in the windows as it approached the gate. The
bar was directly across from it.

"So what'd you mean?" I asked. "You get fired from your job
or something?"

He sighed, surprised, I thought, by what I'd heard from his
voice.

"Well, I quit. I decided I had to move on."

I was watching for my girlfriend.

"I need that job right now," I said. "So, *¿qué te pasó?* You
burned out on El Paso?"

"El Paso's all right. It's not Albuquerque, but it is getting
better. You should come down. You could stay at my place."
He started watching for my girlfriend too. "No, it was a woman.
Romance, love." He wasn't sure I was listening, and I wasn't.
"So I decided to quit."

"*Hay viene,*" I said.

"That's her?"

"Yeah."

"You *are* a lucky bastard. You find two, and I can't even keep
one."

"*¿Bien fea, verdad?*"

"You lucky bastard."

"I am, I know. *Pues, también* she's married."

Now he was shaking his head like I was before he came up to me. "Let me give you my number before you take off," he said. "Visit anytime. Especially now."

"You don't know what you're offering, dude. I may be sleeping on your couch next week. *No traes una* business card or something?"

"It's old . . ." He touched the wallet in his back pocket, and he felt around for a pen in his jacket, and he stared at my girlfriend standing over there. "Don't you think you better get her?"

I followed her eyes as her body pivoted, searching for me in the long, well-lit aisle beyond the darkened airport bar. "Let her find me. She will any minute, watch."

"You're too much." He pulled out his wallet and scribbled on the back of a card.

I was pocketing it as she saw me. The eyes closed, the face looked at the ceiling, her head began saying no. When it stopped, she moved with a huge grin toward me.

Not a month later I was at his apartment. He'd offered it to me for the utilities while he was in Mexico and Central America for the next six weeks. The timing was a magic potion — I couldn't pay the rent on my studio, hadn't in two months, and my landlord wasn't a patron of the arts.

"This here is some view," I said. "You forget the big picture, you know, of where you're from." I held on to a wooden post on the wide old wooden deck of this old plastered apartment, below me the compact El Paso downtown, and the darkened slot that was the concreted Rio Grande, and Ciudad Juárez beyond that, and then the blackened plain of the desert. The lights of the city all around shook like moonlight broken up in a calm lake.

"If this were L.A.," Danny said, handing me another cold bottle of Negra Modelo beer, "this would be Mulholland Drive, and it would cost beaucoup." No cans of American for him, only the imports.

"A *chingo* of bucks, for sure," I translated. Maybe his Spanish wasn't so perfect anymore and that was why he avoided using it—all of us spoke English best, began leaving the other in the house once we were old enough to ride a bike a few blocks—but, though I didn't know why, he was still thinking about being Mexican somehow: Besides the beer, he played Tejano music on the stereo, and a black felt sombrero was on the wall.

"So what's going on with your women?" he asked.

I took a swallow. "Women?"

"The ones I saw."

I'd forgotten about the one at the bar. "She called me once. Told me to come to New York."

He interrupted. "Is she a Latina?"

I wasn't sure what that was about. "De Califas. I think she's *una de los que,* one of those *que* don't even know how we say California. Don't know *ni una palabra* of Spanish."

"She was sexy."

She was a good-looking woman, I remembered, but I hadn't thought about her.

He laughed too loud and finished his bottle, chugging like a frat boy. "You want another?"

I was only half done. "Sure," I said. I gulped mine down as we moved inside, to be agreeable. "My problem is Lisita. You know, *la otra.*"

"She's a beauty, George." He shook his head as he plucked off a bottle cap like this took strength. It bounced on the ceramic tile counter and onto the floor. I picked it up. "She's not a Latina, is she?" He handed the bottle to me, and attacked another with his opener.

Here we were standing, staring at *the* Mexican-Chicano border, and he still dug around for distant labels. "No, *pura* white girl, and not Latina." I couldn't help mocking that word ever so subtly, even though I realized this wasn't a time for a disagreement over something so stupid. "I only call her Lisita. Her name's Lisa."

"She was a beautiful woman, she really was a beauty." He looked at me like he was about to say something important, but drank instead.

Danny was getting buzzed. He was drinking so fast, already almost finishing the beer he'd just opened.

"Does it matter to you?" he asked. "Does it matter if she's Anglo or Latina?"

"My wife was from here. *Pura chuqueña.* She went to La Jeff."

"So this Lisa, who's married, right?"

I nodded.

"You two are serious?" He spoke like he was doing an interview.

"Depends on what room her husband's in."

He didn't even smile.

"It always gets serious, no matter what it starts like."

Danny went for another Negra Modelo without offering me one — I'd barely sipped this one yet — and we went to the living room. It had two wooden-sashed windows on the south wall, and they were open, and wind blew enough for the shades that were half down to lift and slap. There was a big couch against another wall, and across from it the TV set and a stereo system and a few racks of CDs and cassettes and a tall, stuffed bookcase. His desk was a scratched-up dining room table with a computer on it pushed against the wall and under the windows. That was where he sat. I took the couch.

"Pretty comfortable," I said. "You might have to worry that I won't let you in when you get back."

"Use the computer if you want," he said.

"I never write a postcard."

"You're welcome to it."

"I'll probably set up outside on the porch. If that's okay." There really wasn't enough room inside. I'd been expecting a much bigger place, probably because I assumed Danny made big bucks.

"Of course."

"I've never been one to paint outdoors before."

"You'll have to watch out for the wind," he said. The shade puffed out with it. He was draining this next bottle too fast too, though he did seem to be slowing down in another way, sinking into the swivel chair at the dining room table. "It'll blow hard."

"I swear, you're like divine intervention," I told him. "I'm supposed to be getting money by the end of the month. I didn't want to have to borrow money."

"It helps me out too," he said. "It's better if somebody's here. The thieves, they get to the porch, crawl through a window." He got up for another beer. "So what are you planning after this?" he said from the kitchen. "You going back to Albuquerque?"

"*Sabes que,* I really don't know. *La cosa es que,* I really don't."

He sat down again and set the beer on the table—maybe to let his arm rest. He rubbed his eyes.

"So what about you?" I finally asked. "You don't exactly seem pumped about going."

"I guess it's obvious," he said.

"*Pues,* you did drink all the beers."

"I'm sorry."

"I'm joking, dude."

"I am sorry. I am. Oh. Yeah. Well. I'm sorry." Shaking his head, but not in wonder. "It's because of Mary."

66

I felt like that might be where he left it. "Mary," I said. It was all I could think of to say.

"She lives in Albuquerque."

"That's what you were up there for?"

"Well. Yeah. Mostly."

"You broke up."

"It's been going on. We tried for almost five years."

I didn't say anything.

"She was an Anglo girl."

That took me by surprise. Not that she was, but how he said she was.

"All I ever wanted was to get married. I wanted a house. I wanted a couple of kids. I wanted to read the Sunday paper in an overstuffed chair."

"Really." I wasn't sure what else to say.

"I couldn't understand. I can't."

"What does she do?"

"Teaches art."

"She could've moved here for that."

"She likes her job. I couldn't get my job up there in Albuquerque."

I could only raise my eyebrows and nod.

"I'm happy as an editor. I'm good too. But I decided I had to move on. I had to take some risks. I have to do more."

"And so that's why you're taking this trip to Méjico?"

"Mostly." He was drinking more reasonably now. Sips. "Be a man."

"Be a man?"

"Yeah. Have adventure. Stop thinking like a soft editor. What I was didn't work, you know. It didn't work out."

"You'll meet another woman. I'm sure of it. You can't miss."

"Yeah, probably. Maybe when I'm down there. A woman from my own culture."

I sipped some beer. He sipped some beer.

"What do you think?" Danny asked. "You think it's better we stay with our own?"

This all had taken me so much by surprise. I saw how Indian his dark face was—the eyes, the nostrils. The deep, quiet frown. He didn't wait for me. "I love that woman, I still love that woman. I just don't know why she doesn't love me."

What could I say?

"See? I get mad one minute, sad the next," he told me. "You done?"

"I guess so."

I was almost finished with mine, he was only halfway on his. He carried them into the kitchen.

"I got a futon in here," he said at a closet. He took it and two sheets and a blanket out for me. He went into his bedroom and came out with a pillow. "I'll be getting up early in the morning. Finish packing, make a couple of phone calls."

I unrolled the futon and threw one sheet over it. The wind was blowing with a gritty howl and whistle. I loved the sound, its invisible power and beauty. It reminded me of what I missed about El Paso. The simple things. Sun, and moon, and stars, and dirt, and wind. Day and night. Before I turned off the lamp, I grabbed the pillow he'd put on the couch: I couldn't believe how filthy it was, so much so that its dirty gloss bled through the white pillowcase. I didn't even want to put the back of my head on it, so I used the blanket for that instead, and pulled the other sheet over me.

It was early in the morning when we got up. Too early for me, but I didn't say so. I rerolled the futon and folded the sheets and the blanket and put them in a pile on the couch, pillow on top. Danny packed and I read magazines. He had every magazine

in print, months of them, three big piles. It was what he was
going to do, write for these magazines, and he'd studied the
market. He'd bought cushioned nylon bags for his camera and
lenses. He worried about his laptop, using it, losing it. He needed
to make some calls at his desk, the table. No, he said to me, it's
okay, you can stay. First it was his mom and dad. In case he
didn't come back, he told me, if anything happened. He called
his sister and his brother. He talked to each of them for a long
time about his career. He sounded confident, self-assured. I
wanted to leave, take a walk, but I didn't want him to worry
about me, because I was driving him to the airport. He was
worried about so much. This trip, which so many people I knew
had taken, worried him. His flight was to Mexico City, where
he was meeting up with a friend, and then they'd travel in a jeep
together. The city worried him, driving through the country
worried him. I sat on the couch for a long time, reading, studying photos, while he was in the bedroom. He was a long time in
there. When he finally came out he asked me if I was ready.
Everything but the ticket, I said. He had most of his belongings in a backpack. I carried a small tote down the apartment
stairs—we were loud, and it echoed on the hardwood floors—
and we stopped for Mr. Palacios. I'd sort of met him the day
before, when I got here. The old man had opened the door and
asked if I was looking for someone. He knew everything, Danny
had told me. He saw everything, every coming and every going.
He liked to talk. As we got to the bottom of the stairs, near his
door, it opened and Danny introduced me. He explained how
I'd be staying there until he got back. Mr. Palacios nodded.
Andale, bien bien, ni modo, mucho gusto. Though I knew we weren't,
I asked him if we were related—the same last name and all. He
didn't think so, he told me. He was born in Parral. No relatives
here except his wife. I knew we weren't, I said, I was just joking around because we had the same last name. He went on,

not reacting. She'd had two children previous. They'd had one, a man with a family of his own now, and lost one. We have to go, Danny interrupted. Down the front building stairs, and we tossed his bags in the back of my pickup. We got on I-10 and headed for Airway Boulevard. It was warm out, but the wind was still blowing, so the windows were only cracked.

"I wanted to call her. I had this overwhelming urge to call her."

"It'd be all right if you did."

"I wanted to tell her. I hate that I can't talk to her. This doesn't even matter, I still feel the same for her. I wouldn't even go on this trip. It isn't what I want. I wouldn't need to go if, you know, if we were together, or going to be."

"You should call her, dude. Call her from the airport. You'll have plenty of time. I'll bet she'd like it."

"I just can't."

"That's not so bad either. Maybe you shouldn't. But, *sabes que*, it'd be okay if you did. You guys were together what, five years?"

"I wanted us to live together. An apartment for a while. I wanted her to live with me. I thought she'd agree to that."

"But she didn't. Well, you're both working. Distances. *Es bien duro.*"

"Tell me what you think about this. That in all the time, in all that time, she never once told me she loved me."

I wanted my window down anyway. "That's, well, I'm not sure what you're saying."

"That she never did. Not once."

"But you guys were together a lot? Went places?" My real thought was about sex.

"We had *great* times. Especially the first years. Lots of fun. We loved being together. And I know she did. I know. It's why I don't understand."

"Well," I said, "I think you should make the best of this trip. Get away for a while. I think shaking it up is good. And, *de todos*

The Pillows

modos, you told me how you can get jobs everywhere. This either works out for you, or you get another good job after you get back. Either way, dude."

I double-parked near a skycap booth for his airline. We said good-bye to each other hurriedly, shaking hands.

I slumped onto the couch when I got back. I was sleepy and didn't want to start working yet. I lifted up the pillowcase and I looked at the pillow again. Dead was the only way I could describe it. It once had silky, blue stripes, and then I remembered, with sudden clearness, having a pillow exactly like this when I was maybe ten years old, even younger. It was my favorite pillow. It was probably my mom's first. She'd given it to me when she got a new one, or when one was ruined and she bought a pair. This could be the same pillow, decades later. I went into the bedroom. His other pillow was a match. He had two of them. Two dead, decomposing pillows, discolored not by stains or misuse but by age, the passage of time. He'd been given them, by his mom, and they weren't torn, and he kept them. He didn't notice how black the white stripes between the blue had become, how gray the blue ones. He'd had them so long, for so many years, and he'd kept them, and couldn't see that they needed to be thrown away.

The couch, if comfortable, was old, unattractive, indistinctive. Not damaged in any way, not a tear, not a spill, but it hadn't been cleaned ever either, and it was turning brown, a black film on the armrests from the oil of human hands. Everything in the apartment, it occurred to me, was like the couch. Furniture that functioned but was never more than functional new. Never beautiful, never worth taking care of, not worth paying attention to but for the function. Like particleboard with paper veneer, it would never be "antique" or "kitsch." And all of it brown like the walls, the ceilings, like the shades. Nothing with brilliant color. Not a red, not a white, not even a faded bright color.

Except for that sombrero, the walls were empty. Not a picture, not a tacked-up poster, nothing.

I imagined his Mary on the bed. She is passionate, wanting, in the throes. I imagine her body all alert, hear her breathing fast, feel her perspire, and she reaches, climbs, and peaks. When she is spent, as she drops back into time, naked, her blood still rushing, when her head—eyes and nose and mouth—rests on one of these disgusting pillows.

The two pillows I bought at the department store weren't the cheapest, but close. I liked them. The covers had a satiny sheen, in a pattern of long-stemmed, leafy flowers. I went ahead and bought a set of sheets with pillowcases too. The clerk put them in the biggest bag I'd ever been given. The pillows were plump, overripe, bursting. The front door of the apartment building was locked and the key to the apartment didn't fit. I had to ring the bell. Mr. Palacios came.

"You don't have a key?" he asked.

It felt like the bag barely fit through the door. "I guess he forgot."

"It's only locked at night."

"You think I could get one from you?"

Mr. Palacios wasn't sure.

"You don't have an extra?"

"I'll have to ask Mr. Nevárez, the owner."

"I'll pay you if you want." I reached for my wallet. I took out five dollars. "When you get a chance."

He took the cash. "New pillows," he said.

I swore he wanted to open the bag and touch them. I swore he wanted to talk about these new pillows.

* * *

72

"Look at it this way," I told Lisita. "She's either an artist or she teaches it. So she loves beauty. She lives for the idea of beauty. She *desires* it. Can you see what I'm saying? What other reason to be in art?"

"Why do you suppose he hasn't tried to make it better?"

"He told me. He thought of this place as temporary, and five years later he's still here."

"Is he a good-looking man?"

"He is. And he's in good shape. He's athletic."

"Those *are* the worst pillows I've ever seen."

"I can't imagine a woman getting in a bed with those pillows. I can't imagine a woman wanting to, even to take a nap."

"It is an awful bed." She rocked up and down on it. "How are we going to sleep on it?"

"But you see what I'm saying about beauty, right? Don't you see the conflict? Say she has this lust, this sexual passion, which is the raw form of what drives us into art in the first place, and she's here, with these pillows, in a place, a situation if you think about it, that is absent of what she deeply wants and loves most."

Lisita had stopped listening. "How do you know they were here all the time?"

I hadn't even considered that.

"It's a bachelor's pad. You're being hard on him. He's a guy."

"*Pues*, I'm a guy you know."

"Palacios." She was still on the bed. She was waiting.

"What I mean . . ." I stopped for a few seconds: Lisita was so uniquely sexy that it caught me once in a while. She was pure want of woman, something powerful and undeniable and not visible. "*Lo que digo,* I mean I don't go around saying this all the time. I've never worried about pillows before."

"I care about pillows. You're right about that. Women care more about pillows than men. I like these ones you bought."

"*Quelá*, mommy! I'm talking about *beauty*. That I never realized how much I take it for granted in my life. Put it this way. I want a woman to like getting in my bed."

"Shut up about your women."

"It's not what I'm saying."

"Oh, Palacios."

"What I'm trying to say is that lots of men don't know about women. That a woman won't fall in love with a man that doesn't care about beauty."

"Oh, Palacios," she said, crawling up on the bed. "Are you going to get on this bed with me, Palacios?"

I don't know what I loved most about making love to Lisita. What I think of is her face. That punishing shock of desire all over it. So pleasurable it scared her. I loved making love to her, loved making her love it.

"I'm leaving these pillows," I told her afterward. "I don't think I should leave the sheets though. I don't want him to . . . well, you know, and I don't want it to seem like a personal thing."

"He could've put his best ones away."

"I'm thinking he'll see these new pillows . . ."

Her fingers traced the small of my back and the top of my butt and she sighed as her breasts pressed against my chest and she kissed my neck, under my ears, to my lips. "I love being with you," she said. "I love it too much."

It was early evening when we got out for a drive. I took her over to the neighborhood, by Austin, the high school Danny and I went to, and I stopped my truck across the street from where I grew up, a stone house that was painted white when I lived there and had been repainted pink. Lace curtains in the windows. There was a cherry, stock '64 Impala on the front yard, a Corolla in the rutted driveway. The house was so much like all the others, and as still as a photograph twenty-five years old. I was full of this selfish pride, full of a private joy about our neighborhood, about our culture. I lied. I didn't tell her it was my house but that it was an old friend's.

The next three days we drove under that desert sun and sky, moon and stars, in the wind and air. We drove up the river through the cotton fields and ate *rellenos* at Chopes and swung back and drove down to the San Eli mission, smelling the burning skin of green chile all around. We ate at Kiki's and Delicious and Lucy's and we walked El Paso Street across the bridge and onto Juárez Avenue and we drank at the Kentucky Club. We hiked, until we were out of breath, up a loose rock path in McKelligon Canyon to a high point where my dad buried our dog when she died, in a grave heaped with boulders, protected by agave and ocotillo. We drove slow past the brick house over by Washington Park where my wife grew up and where we'd lived together with her parents those first years. I'd wanted to go, get away, so bad.

And, like those first days, and the others when she flew down, it was the bed, my sheets, with the pillows. Her breasts and waist and hips, nipples, lips, *lengua, nalgas, panocha*. Never enough.

"It's so wonderful here," she said. "El Paso is such a sweet town. I could live here. We could live here."

I didn't say.

"I love you," Lisita said. "I want to be with you," she said.

No, I decided not to. Not for the obvious, that he'd be offended, that he'd take it as a personal criticism. Which would be bad after he'd been so generous to me. No, that wasn't it. It just seemed like too much for him to suddenly learn. Not the embarrassment of realizing that he'd been sleeping on disgusting pillows, even offering them to guests. Much as that might be too much too. But no, it wasn't that. It was if he did see it as I did.

The revelation of the repulsive truth. And yes, I did believe it was absolutely true, an easy call. I did. He would look at these new pillows, and he would look at those dead ones, and he would think of the years that had passed, how he'd wasted so many, how simple it might've been and how he'd messed up. No, I didn't want that responsibility. I didn't want to be the one. I couldn't be sure how he, how anyone, would take it, would respond.

I had to get them out of the apartment and into my truck. At first I thought of dropping them from the porch, then picking them up from the side of the house. Which would have kept Mr. Palacios from seeing me go down the stairs with them, unless he saw what I did do, and that would be much worse, much more memorable. I already worried that he would tell Danny about the pillows anyway. The day you left, I could hear him say, he bought these two pillows that he carried upstairs in the biggest sack I ever saw. After six weeks, I'd learned there was no telling when he might be awake, and when he was awake, and he heard, he opened the door. Though he didn't need to open the door every time. In the afternoon to early evening it was usually already open. He had the TV on, a Mexican station blaring. I worried about walking them down in the middle of the night too, because I didn't want him to rush out and open the door then either. In my stocking feet, down the hall and the stairs and out the door? Unless he saw me, and with the pillows. He'd cracked it open on me between two and three A.M. a couple of times. Once he'd met Lisita, he asked me about her every time I came down without her, which had been most of the days I'd been staying in the apartment.

I was making it too big a deal? Exaggerating the possibility of Mr. Palacios seeing me? If I did, I did, and anyway I finally figured it out: I took the clothes out of my suitcase and put the pillows in and zipped it up. I walked down the stairs.

I heard the door opening.

"Moving out?" Mr. Palacios asked.

I kept my hand on the suitcase handle, but rested it on the floor. "Daniel's here tomorrow night. He's taking his apartment from me."

"Tomorrow night?"

"Yeah," I said, "so I'm getting my things out now."

I carried the suitcase to my truck. Left it, and I went back. Mr. Palacios's door was wide open now, and the TV was on. I brought down a couple of easels, my paint boxes. After a couple of those trips, I unzipped the suitcase and took the pillows out and went back to the building with it empty again.

I passed his door and up the stairs and when I looked behind me I saw him standing under the threshold watching me go up. I made two other trips. Then I repacked my clothes in the suitcase.

He was standing at his door, suspicious.

"You forgot something?"

I acted guilty. "Yeah," I laughed.

Now he watched me more carefully. A few hours later, when I was moved out, I cleaned up what mess I'd made, and I locked the door behind me.

"You mind giving him this key when he gets here? He told me it's a spare, so he can get in with his. And here's the other too."

He looked them both over. "Tomorrow night?"

"He's supposed to be here tomorrow night."

We both waited.

"Well, it was good to meet you, Mr. Palacios."

About Tere
Who Was in Palomas

Guillermo Santillán didn't like the

nickname Memo so he was Willie. He pronounced it "Weee-lee," you know, like popping "wheelies" on a bike. He liked to say he was from Mexico, or sometimes Nuevo Méjico, and sometimes *pinche* Tejas. He was just from Canutillo, living out of an old adobe. It was square, four sides, and three windows, and a door. The plaster on it was falling off and it wasn't so it would look real hip but just that it'd been there a long time. The man who owned it, who Willie was renting it from real cheap, he poured the cement floor himself, so the inside wasn't plain dirt no more, and it had high and low spots and cracks. He stood up two stud walls and drywalled them — he never got around to the taping and bedding part, just nails and seams, hammer marks — to make the bathroom a room and then the bedroom a room. No door to the bedroom. The whole house was so dinky that when you opened the front door — which was hollow, a fist could go right through, but it was a lot cheaper that a solid door — and stepped in, *pues*, you were on the other side of the house.

Willie got to living there with Teresa Gámez. He was in that kind of love with her that he also hated her. He didn't trust her, didn't like how he was about any of it. He didn't want this love. She was married to a person who was so ugly. Willie wouldn't even call him a man. He stunk like an alley winos piss in. He plain stunk. When this person walked, he slumped like a *tecato,* but he didn't do no *chiva* or *roca* or meth, he wasn't a sniffer, nothing, he just drank beer and smoked *grifa* and didn't do nothing for work except sell some to other stupids. No, it wasn't just Willie who thought this way. Everybody asked how could Tere be with such a person. Something about her past, something wrong about her. And so something he didn't trust about her. It wasn't like everyone didn't talk the same thing. Like about that body of hers. That figure. This person, her man, he didn't fight Willie to keep her. Willie offered her a place to stay, *y ya,* she was there. But how come it took her so long, and then how come she came over so fast? He hated how he wanted her and how he had her. Even after she moved in and lived with him in the adobe, which he got *nada más* because he was passing through and it was cheap and the dude who rented it to him gave him some work. That was Willie. Passing through. So he was scared of Tere. Then after a while she told him she was leaving him, going back home to Palomas. Fucking good, he said. Why? he asked her. She was crying. So leave, he told her. Just leave. She left.

So he left too, and now he was talking with this woman and they were at a Mexican restaurant and he wasn't going to tell her one thing about Tere. He didn't tell his cousin, he wouldn't tell this *gringita.* Nothing about how he loved Tere so much his muscles clenched the air out of his body and his heart and like he couldn't breathe, and it made him sick like a flu.

He and this Irene—Irene Something, he couldn't get her last name—were done talking about the three weeks he would baby-sit her house. She liked to talk, this woman. She was going to France and Spain, which yeah of course he knew about. But no, not about Hemingway or Cervantes, or Matisse or Miró, Prado or Louvre. He'd been to L.A. and Phoenix and Vegas and took planes to get there. No, he didn't really like to drink wine. Yeah, he loved New Mexico, he agreed with her, nodded his head at the same time he said yes. Then they were done talking about these jobs he planned to look into, which was what he told her he was doing, and when there was no more gossip about his cousin Jessica, who worked for this Irene, they didn't have too much left to say to each other.

"Yeah, it's all right here," he said. The restaurant chairs weren't easy to sit on, and he wasn't hungry.

"So many people get here and can't ever leave," she said.

"If you want to stay and you can, I guess no reason to go."

"Are you next?"

He phony-laughed and shrugged. "I don't seem to stay in anywheres that long."

"Maybe we can change your ways," she said. She played with her voice like her fingers did the airy, shoulder-length hair on her forehead and neck.

They finished margaritas as their waiter turned the corner. He wore high-top hiking boots and old jeans and a restaurant logo T-shirt, sleeves rolled up to show off matching, bracelet-like tattoos on either side, a gold stud earring, and moussed messy hair. He was cool in how he moved and talked too. They each said yes, they would have another, frozen, salt. Irene made winks at Willie while the waiter first listed the sauces she could choose for her enchiladas and then the kinds of beans she could select to go with them.

"You're probably not used to that," she said.

"It's that we always order like enchiladas and they come with frijoles."

"Mexican food is totally big here," she said.

"Hey, I'm not complaining."

"You're probably used to the best Mexican food."

"I dunno. It's like food, if you know what I mean."

"Probably people would want to go out to an American restaurant."

"Yeah," he said. "Like a Luby's cafeteria. You know, hot rolls, meat loaf, mashed potatoes and green beans, and coconut cream pie."

She laughed real. "I live close. Just around the corner."

"These drinks are pretty cheap, so I'm sure I'll like the food a lot."

Hers was a pretty two-bedroom bungalow in a rich, green neighborhood, oak trees tangled up in it, squirrels scratching the tar-shingled roof. Her tour took him over the sanded, glossy wood floors, past bubbly lamps and padded chairs and little tables, a double bed, head and footboard part of a set of matching tables and a bureau of a thousand drawers and a vanity with a mirror that was like a wall. Another bedroom made into an office, all the manila-folder-colored machine tools: computer, fax, scanner, printer. Books. Bookcases all Formica white. The kitchen was small, sink and faucets and tile the originals, but shining cappuccino maker and microwave and toaster. She was new-mommy bright.

"No," he said, "not exactly my place in Canutillo." He told her that part of his story.

"I bet it was beautiful there. Authentic."

"Yeah, right."

"I think you miss it."

"You kidding? When I get to stay in here?"

"I am really glad you like it. It's my first home."

He wanted to go to sleep now. Willie was sleepy all the time. His body already had fallen into the soft sofa—his bed, sheets and pillows and blanket, waiting neatly. She told him how there was too much light above it, under the picture window. She'd just had that put in, the rotted sliders taken out. The new blinds didn't fit though, and others were being made. He couldn't say nothing. It wasn't moonlight but light and it was bright like being awake and he hoped he could go to sleep, try, she'd let him, soon. She'd turned on the air-conditioning when they'd come in from the restaurant and already it wasn't so hot and he waited on her.

This Irene was just out of the shower. Like all the other rooms, the bathroom was not far from where Willie sat. She opened the door, a thick towel around her, stood in the tight space between rooms. "There's plenty of hot water," she told him.

"It is pretty hard to not get all sweaty," he said.

"I can't sleep if I am." She stood there. "This humidity here. Not like where you're from."

"Maybe I will, *gracias*."

"I left a towel out for you," she said. She was still standing there, holding up her towel where she had it tucked in.

"Thanks," he said. He didn't want her to talk no more. Please. He wanted to sleep but knew he wouldn't right way. Knew he didn't want to talk to this Irene no more. He couldn't. What else was there? He hadn't imagined this part, the days to stay with her before she left and he'd be alone. Her talking all the time.

"Yeah," he told her, "I think I will take a shower if that's okay."

"Of course you can!" Her voice all cheerful and generous. "Well, good night then," she told him. She went into her bedroom, closing that door, the light from her bedroom, behind her. He could hear a radio go on.

When he got back from his shower, he wrapped himself into a sheet and shut his eyes. He couldn't stop it. It was so horrible to him, he hated this so much, but he couldn't stop. He could feel her body fill out like the light coming through the window, like heat. Then she'd be above him, squeezing her *chiches*. He'd feel them in his face. He'd move his hands to the curve of her waist, then to her butt. His mouth would be between her legs, where he could taste and feel the slick *labios*, all her sexual muscle pushed into him. She'd want him inside her mouth. He'd see them both, every angle. He'd listen to her, her sounds, he could hear them in his ears. She'd be turned around, and he'd see her arching her neck and back, and she'd be tasting him with her own taste on him, and he'd be on top, and he'd watch her face, eyes closed and lips open and wet, and he'd see every part of her, nipple, belly button, thigh, *panocha,* and she'd tell him do it to her, a voice, do it to her, loud as hearts, and he'd both taste her there and be in her there and he wanted to break her, *this? this?,* her breasts under him, his hands gripped onto each *nalga* and he's telling her he's got her he's having her he's got her she can't stop him and she's moaning she doesn't want him to stop she wants him wants what he's doing.

It came out on the couch and he felt both relieved of the torment and embarrassed by its strength over his weakness, and because it was mess and it was a pretty, new couch. He jumped up to get the towel he used for his shower and he tried so hard to be quiet both times there and back but the wooden floor creaked under his bare feet. He thought he heard Irene moving but no light or sound from under the door and so he'd been quiet enough and at least it didn't seem like she heard anything.

And all the day he thought of her. Glimpses, nothing like at night, but her when he opened a simple cabinet door in the kitchen. When pulled out a drawer, digging around, her. Bored, he rummaged through the cabinets beneath the drawers, where Irene and everyone kept nothing but the pots and the pans, and he thought of her. He opened the drawer by a table next to the stuffed chair, one with papers and receipts and an address book, as though he could say he looked for Tere's name and number in there and then went through them all thinking of her, trying not to think of her, going through this Irene's stuff. He was awake and he was standing and he was dreaming of her in Palomas without him. It ran from what she'd told him: They had a dripping wall-unit air conditioner, and so it was better inside, and she had told him about touching herself while her dad was away working, when her mom was at her sister's, when they were asleep and she wasn't. It was summer in Palomas and her body would get wet, all her body, until it would become as wet as inside her, where she would rub herself. He had listened to her tell him about this and it made him so enraged with jealousy because he didn't believe her that she was alone and so he would fuck her right then, take her so hard so that there would be nothing left in him to make him imagine.

He wished he could sleep and not wonder if she was already going out. Would her cousins or brothers introduce her to someone else? Every man wanted to get her. Would she have a date already tonight? Would she like to kiss him? Would she let him touch her? Would she like it? He tried to sleep and he tried to wake himself up. How could she go to Palomas? Didn't she say she hated Palomas? Dirt and scratchy weeds and rocks, and rocks, and boredom, *norteña* radio a siren outdoors from the earliest morning until so late. The only time she might like it there, she'd told him, would be if she was with him, if they were together. He started holding her, touching her. They were on the mattress, in darkness, staring. He was so sick of her, of his want of her. The rhythm of he wanted her, he didn't want her. The fever again, this time and that time and no time.

"Mattie's my best friend," she said. It was gray dusk, and she'd been home for almost an hour. "We talk about everything." She saw his expression was not enthusiastic. "We won't get back that late."

He didn't want to go over there with her, but he didn't know how he could stay back in her house without her, not do what she wanted.

"You must have some dirty clothes," she said. "It's your last chance to wash for free."

He did have a few *cositas*.

"Let me have them." She reached out her hands.

Some socks and underwear were in his hand.

"It's all right, you can give them to me." She was smiling again.

He didn't know how not to.

"Maybe you're right, maybe it does kind of turn me on to hold your underwear," she said.

"If all it takes is some stinky *chones*."

She cracked up. "We working girls learn to get it where we can."

He gave her a pair of dirty jeans.

"What about the ones you have on?"

"I don't got any others."

She was really laughing. "Be that way then."

Her friend's house, a Spanish villa, whitewashed and red-tile roof, was a drive only a few blocks away.

"Didn't I tell you?" Irene said. She gave Willie one of the plastic clothes baskets, and she took the other. "Andrew's done well."

"Man, I wish I knew that secret."

She took a few beats before she spoke. "It helps if you come from it."

The heavy front door on the other side of a Mexican-tiled entry patio opened with almost intentional elegance. "Hi!" Her friend Mattie looked like she was modeling the casual clothes she wore. Even the sandals looked sexy on her feet. "You better be hungry!" she said. Irene introduced her to Willie. "Hi!" she said. He pronounced his name and she tried to say it like he did. She had naturally what magazines tried to pose. "Well, Willie, I want to apologize beforehand that we're having a no-meat night!"

"You don't gotta worry about it."

"You're so sweet!" She turned to Irene and winked. "You had to find yourself a dark Latin man."

"He's already got me washing his clothes," Irene said.

"Honey, I'd wash his clothes too."

"You guys are starting to make me feel funny," Willie said.

Under the ceiling of light in the kitchen, Mattie was even more beautiful than in the shadows outside. She had a shape, and long brown hair thick, and hazel eyes set off by an earth shade of skin. Next to her, Irene was bony and no soft bumps, her skin both too transparent and thin, too rough. Her blinking eyes seemed colorless. Around her friend, this Irene had even become jittery, jerky, both insecure and conceited. As she took charge of cottage cheese and salad, a big bowl of fruit, she was mad at them.

Andrew, Mattie's husband, was fat. Not blubber-slob fat, but fat. Overweight in the soft, never was an athlete, never worked outdoors, never been in the military, in that never worked out way. Not so much that anybody'd stare, or even care. Nobody'd notice this guy. He wasn't so handsome either, and here he was married to the sexy woman, and so you saw the fat.

Willie drank bottled dark beer and Mattie and Andrew drank bottled spring water and Irene drank wine. Willie watched a basketball game with this Andrew in a TV room until the clothes were dry and they were all folded real neat. Andrew was into investments, he told Willie. Software and software companies. All obvious now, he explained, but he got there before it was.

"Come wash your clothes here anytime, Willie!" Mattie told him, leaning that body over to look at him in the passenger's seat. She put her arms through the car window and around Irene. "And you make sure you call me before you leave!"

"Isn't he kinda like big to her?" Willie said when they were back.

She did not chuckle or smile. "He's been trying to diet," Irene said.

Willie thought maybe he was messing up, being impolite about a friend of hers. "I'm sorry, I guess I shouldn't . . ."

She seemed distracted. "It's okay, I know what you mean." She headed for the bathroom.

Willie sat on the couch. He could see her leaning into the mirror in that putting-on-the-makeup way.

"You like her, don't you?" she said loud enough, still staring at the mirror.

"Like her? Whadaya mean?"

"That you like her. That you think she's so beautiful."

Willie couldn't figure out a reply. He stopped watching what she was doing in front of the mirror.

She turned toward him, away from the mirror. She'd washed off her makeup. "You think Mattie is gorgeous, like every other man." She walked into the bedroom. "It's all right, I know," she said from in there. "She is."

He had taken off his shoes and socks, and he relaxed his head into the pillow on the couch, and he shut his eyes. God, he was already in a dirty-minded dream, already visualizing Tere naked, and he was talking to her in language he never used to her or to anyone: He wanted to fuck her. He was going to fuck her. He'd say to her, You want me to fuck you? I'm going to fuck you. His language and atttitude made her excited, but he didn't care, though he did like it too, and that he said it and that she liked that he did made him more aroused, but it wasn't just that. It was that he meant it.

Irene came out of the bedroom in a nightgown. White cotton wasn't satin or even polyester, and it didn't have lacy frills at the top or the bottom, wasn't low-cut or designed to emphasize, was not a see-through. But it was a nightgown, thin enough that her nipples were not much of a secret.

She left the kitchen with a glass in her hand, she stood near him for a few moments, and then she sat down in the stuffed chair near the couch and he sat up.

"I'm thinking I'll invite some friends over the night before I leave. Have a big meal for them."

He wasn't sure what she was saying, why she was telling him. She wasn't concentrating on the dinner. He tried to make himself more awake.

"I'm so sorry," she said. "It's orange juice." She stood up. "I'm so rude."

"No, it's okay," he said.

"Are you sure? There's plenty."

"Yeah I am. *De veras*, honest."

She sat down again but on the edge of the chair. "Everything in the refrigerator is yours when I'm gone. It'll go bad, and I don't want to throw it away."

"Thanks. I'll check it out after you leave."

"Squash and tomatoes, and a cucumber, and those carrots. I haven't even opened that bag. I think there are two apples and an orange in there."

"I'll see."

"Maybe I can use the vegetables for the dinner."

"*Por qué no.*"

"You can help yourself now, too, you know. Anything you want."

"I'd feel better about it once I'm alone here."

"You don't have to though."

He nodded.

She sipped her juice.

"You don't sleep in those clothes, do you?"

He smiled back. "No, course not."

"I don't think you should feel uncomfortable around me."

"I'm not," he said. He couldn't help but look. Too much of her skinny thighs were showing because her nightgown, which was short, had ridden up even higher. He didn't let his eyes follow their path though. "You're so nice to let me stay. A lot of help to me, you don't know."

"It's nothing. You're doing me a favor." It was a breezy night, clear, and the moon, in the picture window, seemed to sway between the branches and leaves. "I want you to trust me. I know I trust you."

"Yeah." He had turned his head to see out the glass too, then back. "I like it here."

"I don't trust everyone. I really don't. I don't know why I know I can trust you."

"You can."

"You have pretty feet," she said.

He looked down. "I do?"

"Yes," she said. "They're just right."

"Oh yeah?"

"My first years of college I was in a studio-art program."

"So that's why the stuff on the walls. It's all pretty."

She smiled, sipping her orange juice patiently.

"I'm not keeping you up, am I?" she suddenly asked.

"Me? You're the one who's gotta get up early for your job."

"I don't really need to go in in the morning."

"Take the day off," he said. "You probably could use it to get ready for the trip, right?"

She nodded, but she wasn't really paying attention. "You wouldn't like salmon, would you?"

He bobbed his head a little, trying not to say no.

"I'm thinking I'll make poached salmon. It's so easy. Everybody loves it."

He nodded agreeably. "I'll try it if you make it. I know salmon's supposed to be a good fish."

She made a noise between a sigh and a yawn. "Well, it's probably getting late enough."

"I feel like I'm just starting to wake up."

"Too bad you don't like wine," she said. "I feel like another glass of wine."

"*Pues, ándale.*"

"I'll save it for the dinner. I can't believe you don't like wine."

"It gives me a headache."

"Not good wine," she snapped. "You've probably only had cheap wine."

"No ways," he laughed. "Where I'm from you can get Mad Dog at any corner store."

"Mad Dog?"

"Yeah," he said. He stopped laughing at his own joke since she didn't get it. "Really, it's all right to drink without me, go on."

"I *always* have at least vodka around, but we finished it a few days ago. I wish I had some for this orange juice." She was shaking her head. "You like screwdrivers, don't you?"

"Sure. Hey, if you want, I can go out and get some vodka for you."

"I usually have some around. Some gin too for a while." She took a little time. Adjusted the top of her cotton nightgown. "I should go to bed."

He didn't say nothing.

"I guess I've had too much wine tonight already," she said.

He yawned unintentionally.

She stood up, lingered. "So, see you in the morning."

"You're chickening out, huh?"

She waited.

"Not ditching school."

"Oh," she said. "No, I better go in."

"Do you mind if I take a shower?" he asked.

"I should," she said, "but I'm not going to."

It was his worst night. The hunger and need felt more like numbed wounds, his confused body and mind throbbing with their pain. His dream body became as fuzzy and fragmented as Tere's, shifting and floating. He wanted to talk, use his actual voice. He wanted to hear hers with his real ears and so he whispered, saying what she would say, and he would answer for her. No, he had never been through anything like this. He couldn't stop. He would see her bedroom as he imagined it—a single bed, that bed, a bedspread she told him was the same since she was a child, a diploma above it, a cross, a guardian angel, the Virgin, and then he was ravishing her, she was ravishing him, the lust and desire upside down and rolling around without gravity, floating like dust on a hot night, and they were moaning. He was moaning, almost there, doing her from behind.

Irene opened her bedroom door. He was naked under the sheet, and he was sweating. He could still feel himself, stopped.

"I heard something," she said as she approached.

He tried to shake it off but couldn't. "What?"

She didn't seem right. "I can't sleep," she said.

He was really embarrassed.

"I'm sorry," she said. She lowered her head and rubbed her palm over her eyes.

She'd gotten too close to him, she was standing too near. His mind was still a wanton fume, his heart was going, pushing blood down there.

He hadn't seen her walk off but he heard her weeping in her room. He put on his underwear and pants and stood at her door. "Are you okay?" He was still mostly hard.

She was on her bed, face down. Her nightgown had scooted up above her pearl panties. They shined like silk, and they were cut to reveal. She didn't answer.

"Irene?" he said. "Are you okay?"

She said something too softly so he went in the room and sat next to her on the bed. "Irene?" He didn't want to touch her. He did not want to. He touched her leg. He wanted to be polite because she was drunk. She wasn't sobbing. It was a light, gentle cry. "Irene? Are you okay?" He heard her say yes. He wanted to do what was right. "Are you sure you're okay?" he asked her. She didn't answer, and his hands moved higher onto her, he really was touching her skin now, and then she responded too fast, too hungry, and she cried the whole time, and she kept on crying. He left the door open when he went back to the couch. He could still hear her in there. He listened until it was inaudible, or no more, he couldn't be sure.

He went out in the morning—he really looked for a job—even before she left for her job, before she'd made coffee. It was getting hot. When he got back into her house, he turned her air-conditioning down. He still felt too hot no matter what. He felt bad, like he was getting really sick. He was going to call Tere. He opened her refrigerator and he downed her orange juice from the carton and he cut two slices of her cheese and he went into her bedroom. He got on her unmade bed and he picked up her phone next to the blinking message machine and punched in the list of numbers and Tere's brother answered and told him *que no está, no, no sé donde, quién sabe, no sé donde cuando nada, hombre, nada, boss, nada, y no,* their mom couldn't

95

talk to him. He felt so tired and he put his head down and for a while he didn't notice that it was on her nightgown and her panties. Then it started. He imagined but the need and want were too real. It felt like a convulsion and a scent had become a musk that stained the air. He took a shower and he came back to her bed and he held the phone again and he thought about more phone calls but he stopped himself and opened the cabinet drawer on the end table and he heard something drop as he did. It rolled on the hardwood floor. It was a penny. He wasn't sure where it came from or what it was doing there. He hadn't knocked it down from above. Maybe it was so the door shut well. No, it wasn't that. It hadn't dropped and fallen on the top ledge either, couldn't have. There wasn't even a phone book inside. This was wrong, he knew this was wrong, this was something else bad about him and his life. He still looked. It was personal stuff. In a box was some cash, twenties only, and coins from other countries, and credit cards. Another box of letters, personal letters, and birthday cards, another of photographs. Piles of paper, in folders and not. Finally he put it all back. He wasn't really thinking much about them. He was sick, that disoriented. He didn't take anything, he didn't even think of taking anything, but he knew he was doing wrong. Everything about him was wrong, was bad. He was bad. So bad he was already dreaming about Tere again, dreaming of being in Palomas. So awful. He was so miserable, so wrong, so in love with her. He was worried. Even more embarrassed. He knew it was there still, an animal odor, even though he couldn't smell it anymore. He tried to figure where to put that penny back. He couldn't know if he had opened it in such a way that it fell or if it would fall any time. He locked the penny in on the hinge side, so it would drop again when it was opened again. He decided he'd make her bed. To let her know that he'd been in there. He put her undies on top of the chest of drawers. So he'd tell her he'd used her phone and made a long-distance call.

She seemed to be in a good mood when she came in, earlier than the other days, early afternoon. She had groceries, a few bags with her, and he went for the last one.

"I guarantee that you're even going to like this dinner," she told him when he got back from her car.

"I'm sure it'll be great."

"You don't seem to eat much."

"I just haven't been hungry. It's the heat."

"It's so cool in the apartment," she said. She went in and came out of the bedroom. "Thank you for making my bed."

She didn't say more. They weren't talking right. He felt he would be caught any minute. That she would tell him. It was like he'd done something even worse but couldn't remember some horrible detail.

He came around to her side of the kitchen counter. "I used your phone in there," he admitted. "Made a long-distance call, and, I dunno, I thought I might as well, you know, make your bed."

"And it was nice of you, thanks," she said.

He didn't know what to feel worse about, what to feel the most guilty about, what it was with her.

"So last night," he told her.

You could see her listening to him, heard well, waited for him to finish until she knew he wouldn't. "I was in a mood." She wanted to say something else, almost leaning over with the words.

"Seemed like, I think, you were mostly in a good mood," he said.

"I think I was too drunk."

"You weren't so bad," he said.

Suddenly she said, "Was that all that you did in there?"

"Whadaya mean?" he said. It was shame, complete shame that drained him.

"Did you talk to Mattie?"

"Mattie?"

"There was a message on the machine from Mattie."

"For me?"

"Yes and no."

He stood, no idea what she was talking about. "I don't understand, I really don't."

"She asked for you. Like you were screening calls."

"I didn't even hear that phone ring."

"It sounded like you picked it up once, and then she called again while you were here."

He had no idea.

"She was asking for you."

She'd taken all the food out of the plastic bags. She went back into the bedroom and into the shower and then back into the bedroom again, doors opening and closing too hard.

She was wearing a white blouse, white shorts, white sandals. She did not have makeup on.

"You look so pretty, just your, like, face," he told her.

"Thank you." She didn't even pretend to go along.

"What is it?" he asked, not sure to be close to her or farther away.

"Nothing."

He went into the bathroom and then he went over to the couch and he looked out the window and he was remembering Tere and how angry she was when she left and then he came back to this kitchen where Irene was cooking the dinner.

"So what's wrong?" he asked.

"Nothing," she said. "Everything's fine."

"No it's not."

"Nothing's wrong."

"I'm sorry I was in your room," he said. "I'm, you know, sorry."

For a long time he didn't know what to do and he didn't say anything and she didn't say anything until finally she said, "Willie, I've changed my mind," and as he got his things together he wanted so much to confess about that penny but since she might not have noticed—not yet, or wouldn't ever— he just left.

Brisa

The first time I saw her she was walking on Sunset between the XXX Movie Theater and the Saigon Restaurant. I'd slowed down and stared but she didn't look back and I wasn't sure about her. She had lavender hair, the most beautiful hair I'd ever seen, and as it blew into her face she flicked it to the edges of her eyes. In only a glimpse, I saw this pout that made her lips as sexual as a fragrance. At first I thought she might be a prostitute, even though she didn't wear the clothes and she didn't show the skin and it wasn't a usual spot for them. I circled back once I started more than just thinking about her. She was already gone. I kept driving and pulled it over to ask some of the ladies not that much farther down the boulevard. I talked to a black one who was too young and overbuilt, who almost looked clean because the black leather shined so bright. Her attitude kept me on the subject and so the conversation was short. I pulled up to a white girl who I thought looked old-fashioned in pink hot pants and a polka-dot halter top and long sandy hair. When she came over to my car window I saw rosy pimples and dark roots. Neither of them knew anyone with long, light-purple hair.

For weeks when I drove the boulevards I kept an eye out for her. Most nights I'd make an easy cruise down Sunset. I didn't believe she was whoring, but no way I'd rule it out. She was something special, different, and I'd been thinking about her compulsively. I'd never gotten like this before. So many girls, so many types, so much available, and this one was getting me mean and sensitive. At both my jobs people were saying that I was coming down with the Hollyweirds. I'd have agreed with them if I'd never found her.

When I did she was walking real slow on the other side of the boulevard. Even so, I wanted to get on that side of the block as quick as I could to not lose her, so in the middle of the street I whipped in front of a Corvette, which had to brake hard to avoid hitting me. I moved fast and the driver followed close behind me, real badass pissed. When I'd pulled into an open slot a few car lengths ahead of her, the Corvette stopped next to me, those big headers stuttering loud, and the man with the golden chains leaned one hand onto his empty passenger's seat and spoke that poetry to me. I ignored him like I did the rest of humanity I was ignoring as it passed—the nature freak in bikini swim trucks roller-skating with a headset, admiring his reflection in the glass storefronts, or that thing all in black-and-white face powder spooking toward his dark world, or like the twitchy junkie hitting on me for coin. Who cared if slickboy screamed at me? I cared about him as much as I did the other drivers behind his Corvette busting with their horns, or that bus driver whose lips were for both of us behind his graffitied windshield. The Corvette took off.

"You wanna ride?" I asked, standing on the threshold of my open door, my fingers tapping the roof. I didn't want to seem too excited talking to her, but her eyes were a surprising blue, and her skin was white. It was like neither had ever squinted in sun or wind. She was unnatural and now I felt the same.

But she looked at me like she'd known me every day of her young life and found nothing extraordinary about my asking.

"Okay," she said.

I ducked into my car and popped open the door on her side. She got in carefully and shut the door undramatically. She didn't say anything, but she turned toward me and her eyes made a sketch. Not caricature, not romance. I gushed like a teenager and drove like some old dude horrified by traffic, muddled. I didn't want to just drive around and didn't want to take her to some motel and I didn't want to go to a club but I was afraid if I didn't get it together right then—I didn't want to waste this chance for some other time. I drove west.

"So what's your name?" I asked finally.

"Brisa."

I didn't believe it was her real name either, but I wasn't going to fight her about it. Even her blue eyes didn't look honest.

"That's Spanish," I said.

"Yeah?"

"Are you Mexican?"

"What's the difference?"

I waited for her to say something more, to ask questions, and so we traveled in silence. It made me uncomfortable. She seemed unconcerned.

"You wanna get a *trago*?" I asked. It was a little language test.

"I don't think they'll let me in any bars." She smirked. "I'll smoke whatever though."

"I didn't bring nothing."

She shrugged.

"I can stop at a liquor store."

She shrugged.

I bought a pint of Southern Comfort and broke the paper seal in the parking lot. I politely offered it to her first, and she took two decent, familiar swallows. I was impressed. "You're all right," I told her. She gave me back the bottle and a simper.

We drove around for a while. I told about what I did for a living, and she liked it, especially my second job as a bouncer. She seemed to get more interested in me. I can't say I didn't want to know more about her too, but I didn't want to spoil what was looking pretty good. So I didn't ask her how old she was, if she was a runaway, if she had any habits, where and who she stayed with.

"Let's go somewhere," I suggested.

"Okay."

"My apartment?"

"Sure."

I'd never taken anyone from off the boulevard over to my apartment. It was something I didn't do for man or woman. She was an exception.

And there was nothing to it. We were in bed. I didn't coax her, I didn't have to persuade her or reassure her, didn't have to play anything. For her it was like getting in my car. She moved out of her clothes and onto the bed and she let me hold her and touch her and have her. Her eyes would open one minute, close another, and it was like we were cruising Sunset. I was part of some dream she was sleeping through.

We stayed in bed for hours, until cats cried like babies, police cars squalled like cats. In the morning I told her I'd drop her off on my way to work.

"I'll stay if you want," she said.

I didn't want her to disappear, but I was afraid to let her. "Maybe it'd be better if you didn't this time." If she'd had asked once more, if she'd showed any sign of irritation, I'd have let her stay.

"Okay," she said indifferently.

"You have a place I can find you?"

She looked at me with that smirk of hers. She wrote down a phone number.

I dropped her off on the boulevard, at a corner she wanted me to.

"You sure?" I asked

She nodded her head.

"Well then. *Nos watchamos, pues.*" Still looking for something else in her, a reality that I could recognize. "I'll call."

She started up the sidewalk.

"Wait a minute!" I yelled.

She came back, no hurry.

"I'll call you, or you can call me." I gave her my phone number.

"Whatever," she said.

I drove away knowing that this was more than different. I felt detached from the women in front of the sleazy motels who rocked themselves nervously, snatching at the twists of eyes that passed. I jerked around a smelly new RTD bus and ran a red light. I turned up my radio.

In the beginning, what I didn't want to know I didn't ask about, and then, once I got used to her mystery, I made that into a source and sign of strength in me. I was living out a rock 'n' roll song. Not knowing, not asking questions, was a power that made guys shake their heads at me while inside I thumped like a gorilla. It was a brag when I told them I just dropped her off at the same corner each time, just like she wanted. I did have her phone number, and she had mine, and we talked, or mostly I talked. I'm private to everyone, but to her, I gossiped, all worked up like she was more interested than me, and I confessed, made words of all my weak wants and worries I don't like knowing about myself. Early along, then, I think I might have admitted to her that I loved her if she'd asked. Since she didn't ask, I didn't have to think about it very much.

She became part of my routine. I'd managed to get her regularly into the club — I worked the door for security on the weekends. She was hard to not want around. She must have glowed some animal sign because males couldn't deny her, even though, we in management learned, she was sixteen years old. She looked it, but then again she didn't. Mostly didn't. You could say she looked extremely young for her age. That had something to do with the style and tone of her talk, though she seldom said much until she was drinking. Everybody'd sneak her drinks at the club, and I guess, in that atmosphere of live music, dark lighting, and ice cubes, that's why her stories started coming out like they did. She never told me these stories when we were alone. It would always be around a few guys and maybe one of their women, and she'd tell them hard, with this macho smirk of superiority and aggression. It'd usually be about sex. The one that was the most famous: Her father, who she said wasn't really her father but she called him that, the one from San Berdu, made her take a Harley ride with his best friend. She didn't want to go but this father wasn't giving her the choice. The best friend said she'd have fun and to relax. So she did. Afterward she told this father she liked it and wanted to hang out with them, and the two men laughed. Her mother wasn't supposed to know. So she hung out with them, and one day all these biker dudes took turns. Each one gave her a hickey, and when it was over she had an X that started at her shoulders and ended at her hips.

It was stuff like that, told openly besides, that got everything more confused for me than it already was. She was beautiful in all the magazine respects males consider the female beautiful, and exotic, even before the lavender hair. She was pretty. I don't know how to describe how it was waking up beside her and touching her and holding her — love? — but then holding back, fearing the sentimental process, possessing. I mocked feelings, I took positions, I staked claim in skewed ways.

"When I'm not around, do you make it with anyone else?" I asked early.

"Not now."

"Now?"

"I won't see anybody if you don't want me to."

She said it with that indifference of hers. I couldn't say what she meant, and I was teaching myself to slough these feeling things off.

"It's your life," I told her. "Just don't give me any disease."

We did drugs and had sex and more liquor and had sex and went to more and more parties. This one was after a gig by Sweet Billy y los Gordos, a newly recorded band from Texas. There was tequila and hard grains of cocaine and, though it always did anyway, it especially came up with her around, and the subject got specific. Sure I was drunk and high, but it was also how I trained myself to be with her. I said, "It's your life. Whadu I got to do with it? As long as I'm first, it don't matter to me if it don't matter to you."

The next morning I took her to breakfast at Norm's. It seemed like she was drawing too much attention and I felt like a pimp. She ate without noticing that, without saying anything, without acting any way new. She ate fruit and toast, cleanly. I couldn't down the eggs and hash browns I ordered and the coffee tasted like bathtub water. When we got back in the car I pulled out codeine pills from the glove compartment and offered her some.

"I'm okay," she said.

I shook my head in disbelief. "You sure?"

She nodded.

"Honest?"

She made that smirk at me. "Yeah," she said, defiant.

That was when I let go. I accepted my own celebrity status at the club and I listened with Hollywood Boulevard dispassion to her bragging, always like some dude's, about her past, about being raped at twelve and being pissed about that only because she would've done it without a struggle, or the present, about the guys who were trying to put the make on her when I wasn't around, like this kid she went to school with —where on occasion she did go—who wrote her love notes. "Pop his cherry," I'd mouth. "It'll make his pimples clear up. Tell him you love him too, you never know around here if his old man might be rich."

Brisa was beautiful. I knew that shouldn't matter. She was young and, despite all she did and said, innocent. I wanted normal things for her, with us, I wanted to make her happy, really I did. So when she said her mother, who had become a committed servant of the Lord, asked us to go to a church service so she could meet me, what could I say? I agreed to that strangeness out of my infatuation for her.

It was her idea to get high before we went. It was an evening service and the church was short, wooden, and painted white as a dream. Floodlights inflated its exterior and drained the neighborhood of any other color. It was almost the same inside. There was the white of light and brown of pews and Brisa's lavender hair. A preacher was roaring on the stage. Hands were in the air, palms up. Voices cried about touching Him, feeling Him. She and I had come in late and sat in the last aisle, in a corner. She sat close to me, like we were cuddling up in a movie theater.

The voices howled in front of us, hands shaped the body of Jesus. Women cried. Brisa, whoever she was, asked me if I wanted to read one of the love notes from the boy who loved her. I must have said yes. It was hard to look down, away from what was going on in front of us, and it only took a glance to see her own handwriting on the notebook paper. That hair draped over my shoulder, I heard her girl voice whispering to me inaudibly over the wild din of the Arisen Lord.

A Painting in Santa Fe

"Any luck?" Hub shouted above his

rototiller. He'd hadn't seen Jesse walk into the yard until he was almost standing next to him. Hub frowned at the machine, snugged the wire-rimmed glasses around his ears, switched off the engine. "I need a beer. You?" The blue overalls made Hub seem taller and thinner than he was. He and Jesse turned toward the back of the adobe house. "You find anything?"

Jesse wore blue jeans and a white T-shirt, washed and new, the same combination for years. If the high-tops were laced up his feet, that meant work, while the rough-out cowboy boots were for dress-up. He'd been out looking for work.

It was weeks before official spring, and though snow topped the Sandias, the day's sun was warm, and Hub wiped sweat off his face. He was cleaning up, getting ready for planting. Hub and Grace's land, with a view of ancient valleys and volcanic mountains, was terraced over almost two acres, much of it in use: apple, cherry, apricot, and peach trees, raspberry and grape vines, flowers domestic and wild, herb and cactus and even a small lawn. There were turkeys in a pen and chickens and three geese, two propped-up cars, one with wrenches and sockets under and around it.

Grace opened the back-door screen, two cans of beer in her hand. The wide-brimmed straw hat she wore outdoors was on her head.

"You find one?" she asked Jesse.

"He's back here, isn't he?" Hub told her.

"That doesn't mean he didn't," she said.

"I suppose that's true," Hub said.

That Jesse didn't respond was the answer.

"You'll get something," Grace assured him. "We know what an artist you are."

Hub and Jesse took swigs from the cans of discount beer.

"They're making high-rises that look like adobes up there," Jesse finally told them.

"It upsets me to go to Santa Fe," Hub said. "I never feel like I'm dressed right. I feel like wearing a cowboy hat and some long-fringed leather so I look more like part of the attraction than a tourist."

"Gucci and turquoise blend in better," said Grace. "Though I can't complain. We shouldn't."

"On the California coast, it's frothy waves hitting rocks, seagulls floating above," said Hub. "In Santa Fe, they paint those shadows on peeling adobe walls, the baby-blue sky bursting through the thick windows."

"There's good work there too," said Grace. "The Shidoni is a beautiful space and the work is honest and very strong. Those kinds of places may even redeem all the commercial art in the community." She paused there once she caught Hub staring at her and turned, apologetic, to Jesse. "Have you ever been there?" It was a question that didn't need to be asked, but she didn't know how else to move along.

Jesse shook his head.

"You should," she said. "It's really worth it."

"I just remembered," said Hub after some seconds passed. "Lupe called."

"She didn't say something?" Jesse asked.

"She was returning yours." Hub looked at Grace, suddenly thinking there might have been more to it. "I think she was returning your call." He dropped his empty can into a bag full of other aluminums. "You ready for another?"

"Did she say where she was?" Jesse was asking Hub, and Hub glanced at Grace.

"I got a phone number."

"If you want some privacy," Grace said, "use the phone in our bedroom."

Hub and Grace continued to be fascinated by Jesse Molina. He listened carefully and seemed so interested in their world, as though everything he learned was a discovery. They liked this man who had built their home, who'd worked too hard, who'd ran the men he hired equally hard but without loud words, who'd had to be told to slow it down, to take it easy, to enjoy the work more. Hub and Grace wanted their house, they would tell him back then, not so much that it be done fast but beautifully. Jesse had looked at them mysteriously, a muscular serenity, trying to translate the meaning. It was an expression they saw on him often: Jesse working hard to comprehend the abstract, a geometric puzzle. He would stare at the adobe bricks he was laying, or the wood he was cutting, the plaster on a hod—he did everything, seemed able to do every trade well, like a decathlete—and he stared longer to hear better. Around him they felt like Europeans, delicate and upper-class, though Hub was from the suburbs of Colorado and Grace was from urban New Jersey. Then there was the cliché Jesse, the Chicano who suddenly would drink too much, who would do too much of whatever drugs were around, and who'd disappear for days at a time. Twice other women dropped in on him while he was building their house. That didn't matter until they got to know his wife, Guadalupe. It was Grace who began inviting her over for lunch with them all. Grace adored Lupe, talked about how gorgeous she was—a natural aura, she called it—and that's why Grace asked if Lupe would sit for her.

Jesse did not approve, and Jesse said no. Said no firmly. Grace kept asking Lupe anyway. Jesse's just being a macho Mexican, she told Lupe, and he'd get over it, he would understand later. She would paint her beside their daughter, she told Lupe. Lupe and the baby were radiant with earth and life, and when he saw the painting he would understand, it would be like the Madonna and child, she said. No, Jesse told Grace. He took Lupe aside and one day she left and she didn't come back. Grace got so angry she had to compose herself. Hub told her she had to be practical and that they needed Jesse to finish the job. Look at the great work he was doing, Hub reminded her.

Months after the house was completed—the new couches and chairs and a dining room table set, curtains hung over new windows next to freshly painted walls, even towels and kitchen housewares—they had the party that Lupe came to. She got there late, and she didn't have the baby with her. She told Grace she'd seen Jesse drunk in the village, and there was a woman with him. Lupe got drunk too fast, and there was a man, a guy with long hair, a ponytail, a silver earring, leather sandals, and he told Lupe she was beautiful, "absolutely flaw-less," and when Jesse came, when he saw them, when he saw her that close to him, Jesse beat the man, pounded his face, swinging his skull by the ponytail. Hub and Grace let Jesse stay with them for almost two weeks after that. And later he came around now and then, friendly and grateful though he was as mute as ever, until, a few months after the incident, he dropped in to say good-bye; he and Lupe were together again and were leaving town again. She was pregnant, and they were going to California.

"Why shouldn't I?" Jesse said. "Don't I get to see how every-thing is? Don't I get to know if everything's okay?"

Lupe was remembering all the other conversations like this one. "So is it okay that you're staying there?"

"They haven't changed. And she's even being nice to me. Like she always is to you, right?"

"Jesse." Lupe took time as though that would make it easier for her to say. "Jesse, you have to stop. You have to not call me."

"They're my kids too."

"Jesse, this is not about the kids."

"Whadaya mean?"

"Please don't, Jesse."

"Why not?"

"Jesse."

"Do you got a job right now? You wouldn't have to work. Where're you staying?"

She wasn't going to tell him.

"Why can't you tell me?"

"It's not that I can't."

"Is she helping you? Is it her idea?"

"Jesse, I'm a grown woman. I can think."

"And so you think you don't gotta live with me. That we don't gotta be together."

She didn't say.

"I want us to get back," he said. "I'm trying. I want us both to."

"I know what you want."

"Come on," he said.

She didn't say.

"Fuck you then."

He dialed her right back after she hung up. He had to let it ring until, finally, she picked up.

"Let me talk," he said.

"Not now."

"What was so wrong with before?"

She didn't say anything for a long time.

"I'll call later, all right? I'm gonna find a job around here." He waited. "Okay? I might get a job in Santa Fe. I'll let you know. Okay?"

Jesse took over the rototiller. Hub slaughtered and cleaned a turkey. Grace painted steadily in a overlit room—huge panes of glass, skylights—alongside the house. Soon Jesse began cleaning up the acreage of tree and vine trimmings. Grace had stepped outside with a torch and visor. Hub had plucked feathers. A burst of wind caused them all to look up: the mountains, the valleys, the sky. Jesse was the first to go back, piling the sticks and thorny clippings and carrying that pile over to another, larger one. Grace watched him. Watched how easily he seemed to work, effortlessly, the small piles becoming the one large one. Hub saw her watching Jesse and then he watched. It was so simple it was nothing. A pile of debris.

Jesse called it thanksgiving because it was a turkey. But it also was a salad of tomatoes and onions from their greenhouse, sweet potatoes and green beans from the garden. The food was passed, forks and knives and spoons and plates, wine and beer, paper napkins.

"I went to this one restaurant up there with Joe. We were walking, and we decided to have a beer. We get to this nice place, you know, real nice place, with a bar. Fixed up. Stained piñon vigas, Mexican-tile floor, Spanish-style wood tables, Navajo blankets. The building was the real adobe. Joe said it was old, one of the oldest in the city. Well, they had paintings all over, and there was this one. Well, they got a few of *indios*, you know? So this one was of an Indian woman. It was a big painting, big as a window. She was fine-looking, really fine-looking, except she had short black hair, cut, you know, so she looked kind of modern.

Well, she was wearing these beads, Indian beads, turquoise, but otherwise she don't got nothing else on. No clothes. You could just see her. You know, now that I think about it, I don't remember if it showed all of her. All I remember is her top. No, it was from her waist up. Well, you could see her nipples. I dunno, it just bothered me, you know? I mean I like naked girls, and she was looking good. But I said to Joe, that don't seem right, that seems like bad taste to me. He thought the same thing. It was that it was this rich place, for rich white people. That's who came in here, ate at the restaurant and bar. Not the poor people, not the *indios*. You know? It pisses me off. So then I remembered this friend I had years ago, dude I hung with. He was Mescalero. He had this temper, real bad. Like that, he goes. Used to surprise me. Scare me. I got used to him though. So I was telling Joe I almost wished I could have him come to this place. I imagined him having one of those expensive beers. That picture there. I thought, if it's okay for them to hang that picture up there, it's probably okay for him to rip this place up. You know? I told Joe, it's like first they take their land, everything down to all their little trinkets, then as if that ain't enough, as if they hadn't done all the worse shit already, they even make naked paintings of their women. It's like there's no limits to what they can do."

They were almost done eating. There were berries and bananas with cream.

"But the point is," Grace said, "it's art. Art can be anything, of anything, whether you like it or not."

"It's the same people who've been romanticizing the Indian since the West was the West," Hub told him. "And it's almost like you're romanticizing them by protecting them. Since when is an artwork, a nude of anyone, wrong?"

"It wouldn't have been there if it weren't an Indian woman."

"It was probably bad," said Hub. "Of course it was bad. It was stupid, tasteless because it was stupid, bad in that way."

"I agree that a woman shouldn't be used for her sexual anatomy," said Grace, "but if it's meant to be art it doesn't deserve to be ripped up."

"What if it was your women? Your tribe?"

"Art is art," said Hub.

"There are people who don't like what I do," said Grace, "but they can't stop me from doing it."

Jesse wanted to say something else.

"Paint doesn't hurt anybody," said Grace. "It's when someone does something that you can talk about right or wrong."

"Morning," Hub said to Jesse as he walked over to him. The sun had been full up for an hour, but the light was still fuzzy gray. "You going out today?"

Jesse nodded.

Hub ground coffee beans.

"Wasn't it cold out there last night? Bag or no, it was cold."

Jesse had slept on a couch on the back porch, the same couch he'd slept on when he used to stay years before. He didn't like being inside their home at night, bothering them.

"It's too cold!" said Grace, joining them in the kitchen.

"Let me get that rubbish going," said Hub. Grace took over the coffee making.

Hub brought up a tin container, and he held it above the big pile as all the gas clucked out of it. He lit up a pack of paper matches, threw it on. The fire exploded, a black pastel cloud, hissing and sucking.

Jesse hadn't slept well and felt uneasy. He wanted to tell them he was leaving today, wouldn't be back, how he would probably just stay up there, in Santa Fe. But then again he wasn't sure. He wanted to make plans, but he couldn't think well. He couldn't imagine making plans by himself. He wanted to talk to Grace but couldn't see how. He wanted to leave, and he wanted to stay.

"I love this," Grace said, carrying out the mugs of coffee.

Grace and Hub sat down far enough away from the fire to feel the heat but not to have to turn their faces away from it, bundled in down coats. Jesse was standing, his arms crossed and hugging his lined denim jacket.

"Relax, Jesse," said Grace. "Come sit with us."

He sat near and yet a couple of paces away.

"You look awful," said Grace. "You should've slept inside. You're so stubborn. We should've made you sleep inside."

"He would've never listened," Hub said.

"I thought about it last night," Jesse started.

"You should've just come in," Grace said. "You're so stubborn."

"Not that," he said. He stood up, moved up and down on his toes.

"Well say it, Jesse," Hub said after awkward seconds passed. "Say it."

"You're not right," he said. "I don't know how, but it ain't right. It's not. It's wrong. What you say sounds right, but there's something wrong. That painting was wrong."

He was louder than the fire.

"I know what you're saying," Hub said. "I see what you're saying."

Jesse was stepping to the left and right, side to side.

"Okay, Jesse," said Hub.

"Please," said Grace. "Please, Jesse, sit down. Please, take it easy and sit with us."

Jesse did, curling his arms around his knees, rocking like a pouting child, staring at the pile, the mountains and valleys in front of them all, the gold flames and black smoke bursting in the sky becoming blue.

Bottoms

Ixchel, who's always so comforting, she

tells me I'm okay, that I am normal and that I will get better. She is certain of things, smiling and squinting her shadowy eyes at me, those crow's feet the evidence of wisdom she has earned. I talk to Ixchel because I have to tell someone. I remember myself saying, not that long ago, to myself or possibly out loud — one or both — that I couldn't go wrong. I would say, I am on an ocean. That my life is pushed by wind, sometimes calm, sometimes stormy, and while I navigate its current, I don't know its direction. That I am on a ship with sails and rudder and it must be best to not capsize, to steer smoothly. I try to be a good technician and mechanic. I'm sure people believed I was joking around when I said this, being clever. I remember being confident about what I was saying. I could not be disturbed. I had a strong, bright attitude. If the wind whipped with confusion, all I had to do was gauge intensity and ride it through. But watch me now: Wasn't I just stupider then? So stupid I thought I was smart? All that time I lived in the middle of a continent — born and raised in a desert as long and high and wide as most countries — and I knew shit about oceans or boats. The wind blew so hard so much of the time, there was that. You could see how I might have hooked onto my idea. But really, I've only ridden on a boat, in a lake — no, a reservoir, only a fake lake — and never a ship. Once in a sailboat. One of those tiny ones, for two people. Do ships have rudders? Do boats? Do sailboats? I mean, is "rudder" even the right word? I could look it up, I do know it. But that's the point. I never had before. I barely know about lakes. I don't even know about pools, how much chlorine, any of that.

Where was I? Ixchel. Ixchel didn't think my circumstances sounded so bad. That if I got back into work, just worked. She makes sense. I always think she makes so much sense and I do so trust her. I am going to get better. I am going to make it. I am strong and I am not going to succumb.

Though I follow curves that never seem to unbank, my intention is to learn to straighten out, to get along and be simple too. I am tired and I hurt. I want blue swimming-pool calm even if it's crowded. It's hard for me to even walk to my pool. The asphalt is hot, it's a hill up and then down from the complex which is my home, in and out of the dappled light through a shade of trees. My feet ache. I have no explanation for that because I swear I am in healthy shape. Compared to most, I'm sure of it. It's the hot summer. The quiet — cicadas and grackles and hedge trimmers and nail guns — sounds like the heat. I wear a baseball cap because I don't want my face to burn. That sun. I can take the humidity, even like it. I believe in the sweat, because sweat is religious, cleansing and purifying. But not the direct sun. Hide from that sun on the skin. And dark glasses. Though I like the light, the daylight, sunlight. I feel too much darkness in me. I seek light but not an Anglo sunburn.

I drop the book and my swimming goggles because I always intend to swim the laps and maybe will today and take off the sneakers and lay out a thick beach towel on the grass. It is never crowded at this public pool — my pool, I call it affectionately. The smallest children are in the shallow end with their young, perky moms dunking them. The next sizes up play that tag game:

Marco. Polo. Marco. Polo. I don't ever get what the fucking fun in that can be, and I hate the sound. Lap swimmers farther off, touching walls. Baby-blue pool and pale, sticky heat and poky blades of green grass. It is luxury. I don't take off my shirt and I pull the bill of my cap farther down the forehead. I take the dark glasses off to clean them with my shirt. This is such a good life, I say. What could possibly be better? I shake my head, then look around to see if anyone saw me. Am I talking out loud to myself?

My last review appeared in last month's issue and I am not disappointed in it (it was good, really) but with this new novel I am struggling because I don't know where to begin. I'm suspecting it's some kind of test Ixchel, who is my cherished, wise editor, wants to run by me. A favored author of the magazine, and hers, and I am assigned his latest, due ASAP, tomorrow. She needs something, and she wants this review by me. The book is as explicit as I have ever known, one page after another. I have never read so much about cocks and pecs, the hard and soft, big and small. And it had never occurred to me to consider people as bottoms or tops—that is, ones who want it put and the ones who want to put it. I can't say I'm shocked by the novel's details, nor am I particularly bothered by their modus operandi, but I am on alert. A little touchy, if you'll excuse the expression. For example, a man with a stylish bald head, thick gray hairs on his chest, nipple rings, who I find next to me on the grass, who I bet is top or bottom oriented, who I probably would have never noticed before, for whatever reason has made me uncomfortable, in a synchronicity sort of way—he has put that towel too close to mine and has smiled at me. In fairness, this was only friendly, I'm sure, and it's a small lawn we all share beside the pool. Since he's reading a book, he is simply acknowledging that I too am reading one. This is a friendly neighborhood. Yet, even though I'd already taken off the book jacket, now I'm keeping the spine away from his line of sight. I could always move. There's also a woman on the other side of me. Her presence is soothing. It's because I'd put my towel next to hers, though not to engage her, given an opportunity or the desire. I am afraid of raw desire when I encounter it. Though I do wish I could just go after what's available, even potentially. I hate being such a romantic. I want to be a stereotype: Man sees woman. Thinks woman. Thinks tops. Has woman. Satisfies self.

I've lost the story. I don't mean the storyline, which is simple — eight plus or minus characters, gay, male, going through a couple of very hot days in Los Angeles, the usual Santa Anas yawning casually, the catalyst of lusting, each character's narratives fragmented through several chapters, all of them consumed, metaphorically too I think, by penises. But I've lost or never found the deep story and so I don't know what it's about. I told Ixchel that I have liked reading it, even told her how it's turned me on, except that I'm such a pervert I keep thinking of Cata, of sticking mine into Cata's places: I visualize her fulsome, swaying breasts and the sharp cut of her waist and the muscular upturn of her butt when I make the connect from behind, and then her lips and mouth and her face down on me and, well, so on. Oh I miss Cata and Cata sex. When I told Ixchel this I could feel her smiling and shaking her head on the other end of the phone, but what she tells me is that I have to forget Cata, that I have to fall in love with someone else as soon as possible. Not so easy, I don't say. Not so easy for me either, I can't say. Ixchel has shared with me a couple of her difficulties, and for all her toughness, I know how really sensitive she is. I am into this lesbian culture of hers, sympathetic, feeling safe. We empathize with one another about the love of a bad woman. I wonder what she would think of the woman next to me. Her skin, though not pale, has not seen much light. She has sat up and she has pulled down the straps of her bathing suit top to rub tanning oil there and around and then under the edges of the cups. Buxom cups, I note. Very big. Ordinarily I'm not this way, considering in large and small. It is a direct effect of this novel. She is looking at me as she does this. I see her slow down for two beats and then proceed, uninhibited, until she has coated the oil over the entire front of her body to her toes. I am perfumed by the smell of it on her.

A man way too handsome, too conspicuous about it, comes through the pool's gates. He is tall and has a golden hue, evenly, all over his statuesque physique, both worked on regularly for many years, as chic and professional as an Italian suit. He wears those brief swimmer trunks like the gray man next to me, flip-flops I'm sure are designer. He has gold hoop earrings and a silver ankle bracelet. He sets himself up, not inconspicuously, practiced, on a cement ledge, uncollapses a beach chair, adjusts a set of headphones, and places the smallest glasses over his eyes as he aligns himself into the sun. I cannot guess whether he'd be a bottom or a top, but I have to think it now because of this book.

I try to read. I have told myself to get through it fast and then see what I can come up with. But I don't get it, or maybe I'm tired of reading, tired tired, a delirium tremendum of images, trembling with dread and sadness and defeat and lust and desire and love.

"Excuse me?"

I must be talking out loud. I just know I have been.

I look over at her, worried.

She points to her wrist.

"Oh," I say. "Not even three. Eleven of, if you want the exact."

"Thank you."

"Anytime," I tell her.

Shy, I go back to this book, trying to zip through and fight off my eyes from closing. It is so hot I should either take off my shirt or go in the pool. I turn onto my stomach for this stretch of reading.

"Excuse me," she says so I can hear.

I realize she's been trying to get my attention and I sort of slam the covers together in surprise. Am I so groggy or so absorbed? Though not so much that I don't make sure she can't read the title along the spine either.

"I'm sorry to interrupt you again," she says.

"It's not a problem."

"You wouldn't have any change, would you? For the phone?"

"You know, I'm sorry, I didn't come here with a single coin on me."

She gets up and takes a walk and my eyes follow her. A black bikini that fits her despite the fact that she is such a big woman. Huge woman. Gigantic in almost all aspects. Is she over six feet tall? That pretty man is in the water with the man whose towel is next to me, and they are talking like good buddies. Talking about Germany and food. She has gotten some change from the lifeguard and is on the phone. A very quick phone call. When she hangs up she explodes into the pool, swims the distance underwater, and comes up near the two men, who otherwise would not appear so smallish, a wave from her body virtually slapping them. The pool water cascades over her eyes and she pulls her hair back and she stands up — she does this with such an artistic, glamorous confidence. They are all three near one another, in a triangle. The men are still discussing Germany, though now it's not only food but hotels and regions. She does not stay near them in the water very long. She pulls herself over onto the edge of the pool and lies on her back, visually facing that overly handsome, picturesque man. She is behaving sexually whether she means to be posing or not, though I think she is, and yet her presence doesn't even cause a stutter in his conversation. He does not glimpse any

shift of fabric or flesh around the breast or thigh that unavoid-
ably make themselves visible.

Oh I have work to do. I'm determined to finish this no matter the distraction or disinterest. And I do get involved with
the black-and-white text at certain moments. It gets me to fan-
tasizing about fluids and smell and taste. Visualizing. Remembering. I miss having sex with Cata. I miss having sex. I miss
her body. All this while I'm trying to think practically: How
can one use the concerns of this book, in the large, as an issue
that obsesses me as much as it does this writer? A book should
cause a reader to digress, to parallel. Therefore. Despite? I feel
dizzy. It's so hot, and it's so humid.

"It must be very good," he says. My neighbor with the nipple
rings. "I'm betting a romantic story."

I'm too slow to figure out if I am reacting poorly because it is
this book or him. "Well . . ."

"Fiction?" he asks. "It has to be."

"A novel," I say.

"By whom?"

He's a pretentious "whom" word person—though I hope I
haven't reacted as rude as I feel.

"It's just some writer," I say. "I have to read it." I'm fum-
bling physically and verbally, the book on my side away from
him. "I'm reviewing it." I do not want to discuss the book with
him.

"You write? For what magazine?"

I can't think of how to not tell him.

"That's wonderful," he says.

I nod, feeling stupid, both diminished and pompous.

"I'm a writer," he says.

And he stands up. He's become intrigued, and he sits himself right next to my beach towel, his back to the pool, facing
me, smiling.

I have to keep the book out of his reach and distance the conversation about it. "You're a writer, huh?"

"I am," he says. "Or trying to become one."

And the best way is to let him talk about himself.

I look over at the gigantic woman, who has decided to leave the pool's edge and who flops onto her stomach onto her towel on the other side of me. Of us.

"I have already published two books, but I have an unpublished novel . . ."

Or, thus: He's been told by this agent and that one, this writer and that one. And so he's writing a screenplay for it. Both are based on his interesting life. First he was in advertising, the creative side. Then he ran his own restaurant business. He knows wines. He knew wines too well, and also other alcohol, and cocaine. So he left that business. The man who bought it didn't change one thing and now he could retire. But really he doesn't care. He was unhappy then. Spiritually speaking. Dissatisfied. He started reading and not going to therapy but reading about religions. Raised Baptist, and from Dallas, and well anyone can imagine how that is. But with his business acumen and with a growing spiritual insight, he knew others were suffering as well. So he decided to give motivational talks. As successful as that was, and even the book was—a book based on these talks he gave— he was still so dissatisfied. Not that people didn't love him. Almost idolatry. Stopped this too and went more inward, more privately searching. He decided he wanted to be a full-time writer. Next book was still on the research he had done, about religions. When he learns something, he likes to find its practical usage. In truth, it's Eastern in philosophical influence. He learned so much, and he felt he had something to say, but he was glad that he passed through that time in his life too . . . a great movie.

She has been listening to him too. She's kind of pretending not to, and she isn't leaning, not cupping her ear, but she is listening and not staring out there at the pool. She does not see the pool.

Which makes me feel less bad with him, so close to him and me so close to this book. I really do like it that she's there, witnessing.

"Congratulations on writing a novel," I say. "And a movie sure would be great. It'll make you a lot more money than any book."

"You think?" he asks.

It really is too hot, and she has gotten up and dunked into the pool. And now the pretty man is staring at me. He's not visible about it, but I see him smiling at me. He's looking over the top of his designer dark glasses.

"I'll be right back," I tell him. "It's too hot."

I jump in the shallow end of the pool too and I stroke, making curves around her. She has her prodigious back against the tiled cement of the pool, her boulder-like elbows over the edge, her all-meat calves and thighs paddling gently in front of her. I look over to my towel. He has picked up the book.

I wade close to her. "Help," I whisper.

She looks at me like she isn't sure.

"I mean it," I tell her. "Please talk to me. I need you to talk to me so he will go away."

Her giggle is bigger than any woman's I've ever known.

"Please?"

In the morning I tell Ixchel I'm still struggling. She wants me to stick with it. You can come up with something, she assures me. There is not really a need for reviews, there's no special timely importance, we both know that, but she wants me to commit myself and work hard. Since Ixchel hears everything, every little nuance of tone and volume, she too is being metaphorical in her reply. She has a strong mind. She's holding the space for a few more days, she tells me. She really wants me to do this and she wants it to be in this coming issue.

I do too then. Really I do. I only have to be insistent, persistent, determined. No more digressions, no more excuses, broken thoughts, paragraphs, or phrases. That is why these reviews are good for me. They make me concentrate, make me stop thinking and at the same time make me think more clearly.

"Yeah," I say, "it was pretty funny. I probably was overreacting."

"He just thought you were cute."

This is the next day and we both are laughing about it. She told me that she lived close, and I thought what she meant was that she'd walked to my pool too, but halfway to my apartment she said her car was back there. I wasn't worried about it, except initially, for a second, after which I let it go. We were talking, all caught up in it. I'd been telling her about my multilayered troubles, all my confusions, and she'd mentioned something about her husband, and so it seemed fine, all of it, friendly, and nice, okay. A straight line.

"You shouldn't have given him your number," she says.

"He had a card, you know, a real good-looking one, a hip etching on it, engraved lettering, and then he gave me another and told me to write mine on the back, and I couldn't think."

"You really wanted to give him your number, tell the truth."

"I'm not sure what to say to him now."

"Don't return the call," she says.

"It won't be too impolite? What about when I run into him at the pool again?"

"That's true," she says. "Well, I guess the only thing left for you is to choose bottoms or tops."

"God, the world is such a carny," I tell her. "Like, what did you think about the pretty man. You weren't attracted?"

"No, not really."

"How come I saw you like, excuse me for saying this, but practically putting your stuff in his face?"

136

She gasps, both fake shock and real recognition.

"I saw you," I tell her.

"That's embarrassing," she says. "I can't believe you would say that!"

"You should've been embarrassed then."

We're both laughing pretty good as we walk into my apartment. We talk about the books I have around, my computer, and about Cata. It's a photo that takes us to that subject. She's pregnant, but she looks like she's in an ad modeling as pregnant.

"Yeah," I say, "I can't get over her."

"I see why."

"Yeah," I say.

The phone rings and I pick up. It's him. I point to the earpiece. "It's him!" My lips say, "It's him!" She goes into a convulsion of laughter. He's telling me he wants to go to dinner, but it's not about sex, I'm sure of that, it's about me reading his novel manuscript and praising it and him and all that. I don't want to read the novel. And no, I don't want free copies of his guru books. I say, I really feel I should go to a bookstore and buy your books. I really think a writer should get a sale, I say, and you shouldn't give your work away. He thinks that I'm being so generous, but. . . . I interrupt him. Look, I say, I have someone here. I get a little close to the phone. She's in my kitchen, getting over her laughter. I say, look, do you know what I mean? I really can't talk now. But maybe, I say, I'll run into you at the pool soon. Oh, he says conspiratorily. Is it her? he asks.

"He seemed to like it that it was you."

"He's pretending not to be jealous."

"You want something? Water? I have raspberry-flavored sparkling water, cold. Beer? I have a couple of beers here too."

She looks at her watch. "I better get home."

But she doesn't move in that direction. Instead, she gets closer to me. She is too close. So close I suddenly feel the gravitational pull of her flesh, the Jupiter of it. She must be two inches taller than me, she must weigh close to what I weigh. I'm not short, and I'm not skinny. It's not that she's fat. She's proportional. She's just bigger than a very big girl, and every time I look she seems bigger still.

She turns to kiss me. I think it's supposed to be one of those kiss-kiss good-byes. But she's too slow about it, and I feel the heat of her body, I can feel her breath against my cheek, and I have this sense that she's even conscious of her breasts touching me, that she's moving her chest not away or in, but side to side. It isn't that long though, I don't think.

"Hey, well, I'll see you," I say.

"Are you going to be there tomorrow?" she asks.

"Maybe. Although I will have to sit down and start typing at some point."

"You do your work," she says.

Which I intend to do. If I could focus on some aspect of it. Like, what if I were writing it to Ixchel? Dear Ixchel. Without that. Cut that, use it for myself, move along. I don't know how I am supposed to deal with a subject such as this. The energy, that self-destructive energy of desire, that I understand well, too well. Notes, these are, to get myself going. Or just use all the conversational experiences I've been having. The Eastern spiritual and Western screenplay angle of desire. Now I'm losing my train of thought again.

A knock on my door. It's her.

"I had to come back," she says.

I'm caught unexpectedly and I can't think of any reply and I don't think of stopping her from coming into the apartment. She draws me in the flesh of her arms—her real long arms—and her mouth is against mine and her tongue goes inside and my eyes shut as it roams around inside there. I realize, even as this is going on, that I am not responding negatively, I am only passive, up until when she takes my hand and pushes it to her *chiche*—a very unavoidable *chiche*. I leave it there, and I move my hand against the fabric of her bathing suit and I consider reaching under it when I feel her hand between my legs and she stops kissing and starts to go down when I say stop. She doesn't and she is at the zipper saying she wants it in her mouth to taste me.

"We have to stop," I say.

And she does. She stands up.

"I'm sorry," I say.

She looks up at me.

"I just don't want any problems. I'm trying so hard to avoid them."

Her eyes drop, guilty. "You're right."

"I don't know about right," I say, "but I do know about trouble." It's what I'd been telling her about myself for the last two days.

"It's not that I don't love my husband," she says, standing.

"I know, you told me. It's kind of what I'm getting at." It's what I thought our connection was. That we were talking about each other's troubles. Although, now that I mention it, she didn't talk about any worries, it was only me. She'd said she was happy and that he, her husband, was especially happy. She'd described her husband to me. A big man, bigger than her, she said, who was crazy about her, who wanted her all the time. Bigger than you? I'd asked. That has to be something to see. We both laughed. We were, you know, getting along.

That's when the phone rings again. This time I don't pick it up. It's him. He's leaving a message that we are both screening as we stand there. We all three can get together, he says. That would be so grand! We can all go have drinks. Martinis! He is elated by the idea. Call me soon!

Passion, the floweth over of desire, the want to love and be loved which is so raging, that poetry of lover and beloved so often fumbled about in the abstract, as an abstract, as a blustery and invisible wind of yearning that is almost mystical. Like an artist's, or an athlete's. Beauty and conquest. Fulfillment and satiation. The subject of this novel? The theme? Are these men on journeys of self-exploration? Or ejaculation?

It's that I don't think I know what to say, I tell Ixchel. I keep trying. I play around and I seem to get one or another wordy idea and I write down a few profound sentences that appear interesting for the few minutes that I spend with them until my mind starts jumping around and spinning off and then I can't remember, or something like that, and then I think I don't have one simple clue what this novel is about. What the hell do I know about gay men hanging around under tunnels, doubt-torn about whether it's enough to be an anonymous open mouth in the dark?

But could it be that it's only average heterosexual embarrassment that makes it so mysterious? Our average-person shame in our naked body? We don't want to, can't just stand there, our penis achingly hard, metaphorically and whatever, and point, This is passion.

It's that it's not my kind of subject. You want me to review different material, and I do too, because I don't think that because I'm a pigeon I should write for and about the pigeons only. Why not Latin America, or those East Coast Latinos — or, you know what, why not the Americans but with our slant, from our angle? Ixchel is patient. She is listening, scrunching her *morenita* forehead. She's a busy woman and editor with many other complications than me. Her own lover problems. It's what first brought us together. She was in love with this beautiful woman by the name of Catalina, just like me. She is overcoming her love, she tells me. You write another sentence, Ixchel explains, and then you write another. You don't have to write too many words. She says to me, you don't have to understand, you don't have to love the book, you don't have to feel gay (she is assuring me), you just have to write something. Well I know that, I tell her back. I'm not talking about that (I'm trying to reassure her). She tells me she's keeping this spot open. She sounds more frustrated than mad. Usually she's so patient. Or could be she's just giving me the old hard love. She says to not answer the phone and to not answer the door and don't go to that pool. At least for a couple of days, she tells me. Patiently, kindly. I feel bad that I snapped at her there. I didn't need to.

She's at the door.

"I'm really sorry."

She's not in her bathing suit now. Which of course she wouldn't be because it's late, it's nighttime, the dark, low ground insects are cracking loud. It's still liquid with heat. "Pretty dress," I say. The dress would not be called low-cut, but she's so large, there's cleavage up to her chin. I haven't invited her in, and I'm not sure I should.

"I really am sorry."

She has these big, droopy eyes. Has she been crying?

"It must have been that I felt like, because you were talking to me so intimately, that, well, that you liked me. That we had something special."

"I do like you."

"Well, the other like."

I shake and nod my head.

"So we're friends?" she asks.

"Absolutely," I say.

"Okay then." She reaches out her hand and I reciprocate. I feel like I can barely get my fingers around the meat of this hand of hers—her grip is even ferocious.

I shut the door and before I can stop and think the phone is ringing. I don't pick up. I listen to my own voice do its greeting, and then it's a hang-up, but I'm suspicious.

A knock on the door. I open. Her.

"Tomorrow, tomorrow night, I have some friends who've invited me over. Do you want to come with me? It'd be fun. They're the greatest people. And the best cooks. I promise it'll be a good time."

"Free food is my favorite cuisine."

"Yes!"

"Hard to turn down eats."

"Good, then I'll come for you."

I have no intention of going. I probably wouldn't go even if it wasn't that I definitely didn't want to now.

I hate this darkness. I'd rather the hot be a daylight. I'd rather be by my pool sweating, my drainage watering the lawn beneath me and not mildewing my mattress. So exhausted, such a long day. I close the mini-blinds and I turn on the light and I intend to read what's become The Book to the end. I turn my small bed lamp on. I have no idea where I am in it. It all reads the same, and anywhere I read it's as though I'd read it before and not at all. I am swimming. I am swimming laps, back and forth. I am remembering when it was love. I love love. When I was in Cata. It's Cata. It's really Cata nipples. Cata labia. The water is a slick, mucous tunnel, memory, dream, back and forth. Vagina underwater and I'm inside like a fetus and like a man.

She's at the door. I'd pushed aside the blinds to check before I opened it. I was in such a serene mood. I was so untroubled for however long that was. I'm embarrassed that I've gone to bed so early. Couldn't she see that the lights were out? I shouldn't answer, I don't have to.

I click on the porch light.

"I had to come back," she says. She's disheveled. Makeup bleeding at the corners of her eyes like gangbanger tears.

I think I'm asleep, something like that.

"You can't go with me tomorrow," she says. "You can't go!"

I think she might scream and I don't know if I should step outside or I should invite her in. I do neither.

"I just wanted you to go with me. To be with me. To go out with me."

I'm not saying anything. And then she's not saying anything. And we're both standing there, not looking at each other. I don't even hear the static of crickets. Nothing. As though the yellow light works and has scared away those bugs too. And then the phone rings. We hear my greeting again. Then it's "Hi!" of a two-syllable kind and more like three notes long, a scale. It's him. We both start laughing and laughing until we've forgotten anything else and we've said good-night.

Even though I don't sleep I'm up early in the morning, my hydraulic system so much better juiced than the garbage truck out there. I am going to be okay. I'm up to write the review about the book. I will focus on the metaphor of the penis and avoid my sicko and in this instance unprofessional and unmetaphorical lust for breasts and hips and vaginas. I have to stop thinking about it too. Stop that. I intend to send my words over before Ixchel sits down in her office chair. When she punches open her computer, a big surprise from me. I have to dig up quotable passages of the prose, which is what is strong in the work. Usable passages that I can discuss. I don't want to be critical. The writing, I begin to write in my mind, is, if seemingly lurid to some, if overtly explicit . . . where is it? I can't find the book. I know I just had it. I was reading it. Wasn't I? Or I left it at the pool. Maybe I left it and he picked it up. Or she has it. She took it. I know I was reading it. I call Ixchel. That's really dumb, I shouldn't have called her, absolutely no sense, I have no explanation for calling her, for leaving that panicked message. I call her back. I found it. Sorry. Fucking stupid, huh? Talk soon. I put shoes on to walk to the pool. The asphalt not yet hot. I'm fast up then down the hill but it's really early, the gates aren't even open yet, and I'm as fast back. I don't have his number. I don't have her number. Yes I do.

I look around the apartment. I have dirty underwear here and there and dirty socks and pants and shirts that I don't consider dirty everywhere. Books. I'm good about the trash. I don't do that.

She's at the door, and then she comes in, and she looks too, until we are both sitting, me at a chair near my desk, she on my love seat. Now we're just talking. We're talking about losing things and getting upset and being irrational and how these phantoms jump out from the corners, these wiggly paranoias causing fevers.

"It's got to be here in my apartment, I just had it."

"It's that you're wanting to get your piece in, and you're putting all this stress on yourself about it."

"I'm just lonely."

Her smile of sympathy is bigger than anyone's. The biggest I've ever seen. The very biggest in truth, not opinion. I swear she is larger every time I see her. Or I am shrinking?

"You're so cute," she says. "You're such a little boy."

This distracts me from my distraction, and I'm still not one-hundred percent that she didn't take the book.

She's telling me a story about a vacation she had when she was small. Since I don't think she was ever small, I'm suspicuous, which distracts me in yet another way, this music of my mind drowning out her verses, linked nouns floating to the surface: A yacht. A big sailboat. Mexico. The Pacific Ocean. Families. A boy. Her first crush.

I must have tuned back in, gotten closer to this speaker because I heard: Her first crush, and then, She wanted to kiss him so bad. Suddenly I see her sitting on my love seat, in my apartment. She is busting out of a cotton, flowery summer dress, her sex parts enlarging before my eyes.

"I wanted to kiss him on the forehead," she says.

I can't be sure if I have responded quickly or slowly. It's this book I'd been designated to review. It is so many pages of homosexual imagery and then my own personal, private, not-yet-fantasy remembrances of heterosexual behavior that was not only ordinary to me. What can this mean? What implication has a forehead kiss?

"Where I want to kiss you."

It is summer and this is Texas. I get up and check the air-conditioning and I turn on my rotating fan. I'm thinking logically. A fetish? Forehead is symbolic of what? Of body parts above the shoulders, I've never been attracted, consciously, to forehead. Lips. A cheek. Cata was made more beautiful by the bridge of her nose. And kissing her closed eyes. Or it was her neck, the way it fell from below her ears so sleek, sensual.

"My forehead?" I finally ask.

She is right next to me. She has stood up, followed me. Does she know what I'm thinking? Am I talking out loud?

"Yes," she says.

I'm standing still, uncertain, confused. Is the part of my brain that is functioning at this moment right behind my forehead?

She is an autumn cloud blotting out nature's light. My body is pressed against an ungiving wall of Sheetrock as that mass of face leans down upon its desire. Her lips swell against it, her indelicate plucks boring through the skull's thick crust and nibbling at some filet mignon of brain. I am not me. It is not me that this is happening to. The mind, me, I have shifted in space and time, stepped out to observe and record. I step farther away and I see my mind in the middle of a rocking ocean, stars everywhere above, so many stars, too many stars, and planets and moons, and galaxies, all that astronomy stuff. Alone, alone. Alone in the middle of nowhere.

"Stop," I say. She does. "You have to go." I watch her, her steps a little angry as they pass through the front door, and I am right behind her as she does and I lock it when it closes and I rush into the bathroom and I scrub. Blood is rushing to the wound and I know it is swelling and the skin is raw and chaffed. It is throbbing, a blinking red light after two A.M.

I pace and pace and the phone rings and I am sure it is him again and I scream into the phone before I hear anything that he has to leave me alone right now and I hang up. I don't want to be indoors but I don't want to go into the heat outside, not even next to my pool. I need sleep. I didn't sleep the entire night. I remember this now. I couldn't sleep so I watched television and I listened to the radio and then I went back to television. Where is that book? I want to know but I don't want to think about it, about writing a review, about not writing it. About Ixchel. What I will tell her. I'll just tell her the truth. This woman, this giant woman, she came and she sucked on my forehead. And I think she stole your book. It's the truth. This review just wasn't meant to be. Ixchel will understand. She won't give up on me. Ixchel is my spiritual sister. She knows about women and women troubles, obsessions about women, and she knows me better than I do.

I've shut all the mini-blinds and cranked the air conditioner unto a winter chill. I am in bed with my blankie and I am breathing in and out, a meditation. I am so much calmer now. I am dreamy.

My window slides over and the metal louvers clack toward me and side to side and then up. Her shoulders barely fit through, and then she must raise up to fit her chest into the window opening which now in contrast seems so petite. She extends her muscular arms and then this bulk that is her body plunges forward onto my carpeted floor, her skirt falling from her waist, her white thong panties, upside down, like palms together, in prayer. She is in my room, then she is standing up, then she is at my bed, and then she has removed first mine and then all of hers. She has mounted me — I'm a bottoms. As her rhythm intensifies, the book, trapped between the box spring and the wall, clunks onto the floor. My penis feels magnified inside of her. She grips me with those arms, cutting off a normal supply of oxygen. I am smothered by pounds of soft *chiche*. My hands have disappeared into a succulent cream of hips. I hear her breath like the wind at sea.

Snow

It was when his boss called him an Indian that it

stuck. "*Te portes como* some stupid *pinche huevón Yaqui.*" He was only three years out of high school, and it was a job in the city's paint shop everybody envied him for having. It was the boss who had parents from Sonora, who had the face like a mask to scare away demons, who was dark chocolate brown and real short, but he was right to be pissed off and yelling. Geronimo wasn't doing the work he was supposed to, he wasn't keeping up his end. It's that he didn't like the job. He didn't like a lot about where he was, the large and small where, and right then he suddenly got the answer to the big why too. He was not of their world because he was an Indian. It was what he wanted to hear, a secret note passed loud, hours before he was about to lose the job. Except for that boss, and possibly some dudes he played summer league basketball with from Ysleta way back when, he didn't know any Indians. But he didn't think he looked Mexican, he wasn't from there, and he didn't think he looked Anglo, because he wasn't from them, and both were way fucked up anyway, and so he didn't want to be related to either of them. Indian heritage explained it better. It gave him a good night's sleep. He preferred being an Apache like his *tocayo,* the one who was famous. He'd been up there to the reservation the first times when he was real young, with his best friends César and Jimmy and their parents. Fishing in the big lake, stocked with trout, army tents next to the mountains and the tall green pines. He didn't like to fish, didn't really want to eat that trout, but he liked the camping out part, he liked the refrigerator-cold at night after a sunny day, so after the city job was over he started driving his '72 Cougar the two hours up there *solito* until he had a favorite, almost personal campsite. He took a carpenter's ax and hacked off branches and collected twigs and made a crackly fire and ate smooth peanut butter on flour tortillas by it, powdered donuts and *pan dulce* from the day-old-bread store, and went to sleep early and got up at dawn and wandered, watching hawks though at the time he thought they were eagles, and walked besides the tall grasses, the breezes shaking voices out of them, stopped at trickling creeks, which he listened to for so long because he swore he would eventually learn to translate the words he heard in them. His hair got longer, until it was long enough and then even too long. One night on his back, zipped up into a sleeping bag, he was staring at the stars when he saw them, their meaning, and he realized how stupid he was. He was a stupid, a tonto, a kemo sabe.

What he did was ride out, travel the West. He got lost in the Gila and survived for days. Walked in what felt like a hallucination for miles of what all looked the same in Death Valley. He dove into the clear down to your toes Pacific Ocean north of La Paz and, way up the same coast, sneaking onto Malibu Beach. He floated around the Gulf of California, fished for corbina that he did like to eat, and in Mexicali puked up a bad *carne* given to him by a *puta* who didn't like the clean, pretty woman he came into the bar with. On his way to Canyon de Chelly, he picked up a killer girl hitchhiking who only spoke Navajo and spent two days with her. Twice he abandoned blown-up cars— warped head once, camshaft the other—outside Yuma and Deming, in that brown moon desert. He slept alone and too cold on the banks of the Columbia, the biggest river he ever saw, climbed trails northeast of there with bells around his neck to get close to green lakes, where he drank the purest and coldest water, slept with his back against the Blackfeet's Rocky Mountains, the Canadian border. He went down over a mile in a mine shaft in Mullan, Idaho, where he lifted up a sheet of plywood and squinted down a hole so bottomless, wide enough for a man, it was the blackest eye you could ever see. He played poker one night in hotel in Medicine Bow, Wyoming, and won. After he beat the fucking shit out of this dude in Denver—he kicked him in the face when he got him down—and ran, he was shot at near Raton Pass, and he was chased but he got away clean. He had his wheels stolen in L.A., and he stopped just short of stepping on a coral snake in Blanco. He got stung all the time by scorpions. He'd eaten sweet huckleberries off the vine that stained his tongue and lips and sucked juicy *tunas* off *nopales*. Eaten deer and moose and goat and javelina and buffalo. Slept, in mystical Chaco Canyon, below a pack of coyotes who even howled in his dreams. He saw a grizzly stand on his hind legs across a river big enough, *gracias a Dios*, saw a red fox, several bobcats, wild turkeys, armadillos, lots of turkey vultures, real eagles. He drove to Hueco Tanks and climbed the rocks and sat there, until it was way past dark, after his first true love told him she was pregnant, and then a few more times after they were married in the office of a justice of the peace in San Elizario one afternoon—she didn't want their sacred and legal vows in Spanish—and then lots of times later when he didn't have any work. They'd go visit the *abuelitos, las tías* and *los suegros* and *primos* and his *camaradas* and her *comadres* on both sides of the Rio Grande. None of them believed him very much, or else they just didn't like it. He could see them shaking their heads when they didn't say it to his face. So many of them not too happy that he kept saying he was an *indio*—was he joking or serious?—and worried about his beautiful wife and his happy children. When he worked, he worked, but sometimes he didn't, and either way there was never money.

He should have stayed employed with the city? He wouldn't be on the ride, going places nobody and especially not he himself would have expected to be going. If sometimes he wasn't believing himself as he was talking, it was too late to do anything about it and stop. Then, it was happening right up against his eyes, not in his head, not made up. He mostly believed it. There was all that he didn't and couldn't tell honestly and openly, so much he would only tell a few very particular friends — *estas movidas* weren't for children or women or parents, many people shouldn't know. Of course he liked living the way he did.

So interesting! The lady on the plane sitting next to him was gushy friendly, listening as much with her eyes and mouth. He didn't mean to be an interesting native of the Southwest. He was trying to make light conversation, small talk. He hadn't said much of anything. She didn't think so. She'd been visiting her daughter in college and it got her to thinking and talking. She was saying how she was getting older, how the gray in her hair just wouldn't stop but she would not dye it, because she refused to be afraid of the natural, healthy aging process. She was telling him about her life, what she had done when she was younger, and she would shift from defensive to apologetic. She told him about a daughter in college, who, she said, loved what she called the desert region. But you, she said, it's like you have lived a life most of us dream of.

She was sitting too close, squished against him in the middle seat, her breath a gust and her body heat humid. She wore concentric silver hoops in her ears that tingled like chimes. Not one seat was unoccupied on the airplane. Her words were so close it was hard to drop the subject. Maybe it was that she'd gotten to talking for such a long time. Whatever, something about what she said right at the start, about him, made him want to close his eyes. He never wanted to go to the East Coast. The land of those people. He wasn't even curious. He needed to picture in his mind what he was going to do. So he yawned. Sleepy, he told her.

The lady nodded, her feelings hurt. Get your sleep, she said. Much as I wish I could, I never can.

Outside the port window, slipping away behind him, a rainbow belted the horizon, the red orange yellow green and purple, into a deep blue that climbed up to a blue Chihuahua sky, a Navajo blanket. Beneath, clouds rose and fell like the pure dunes of White Sands.

It was LaGuardia when he woke up, New York City, cars and trucks, which eventually he tuned out like he would the sound of an air-conditioning unit in Texas, radial tires on bridges and in tunnels a New Age music, on into the brick and concrete gravity of the buildings, even the low ones high, blotting natural light. Night was not the synthetic black of the vinyl seating in the backseat of a taxi, not a gray of shade in a hot desert, but the pale fuzz of shadow, of whispered deals, of squinting at visions he couldn't attach words to, and sneaking into fantasy places he didn't have the ability to imagine.

He slammed the yellow door at the Port Authority and ran, splashing blackened puddles, down moving escalators, and around the sweeping people in orange highway-construction vests, brooms on the stairs. He was hot in its tall and wide insides. He bumped into a shoulder and another shoulder, and a bag, circled suitcases, stumbled against a baby carriage—people, every angle, every left and right, these people holding plastic grocery bags as luggage, plastic store bags with Christmas presents wrapped in red and blue and gold, faces from nowhere he knew who were cold because it was cold, a wind that seemed chemically treated to be colder still. He stood there and stood there, wearing all of his three sweaters, squeezing his hands, even though he was too warm everywhere else.

She was under a Russian fur hat that warmed her forehead and her ears, wrapped in a plush burgundy coat that reached the black boots. Her eyes, the emerald of glacier lakes, were out in the wilderness, exposed, images internal and external hitting them so fast most wouldn't see how frantically they quivered. They found him: It had to happen. Like birth had to happen, like death has to happen. When she held him, she told him she loved him, told him she loved him so much. I'm so scared, she said. She said, I'm so in love with you, I am too in love with you.

In a cab again, traveling down Broadway, less than ten fingers to Christmas, Santa and cradles, happy children, happy mommies and daddies, babies, a baby, she kept prayer cards on her lap and muttered, counting rosary beads: *Hail Mary, full of Grace, the Lord is with you. Blessed are you among women, and blessed is the fruit of your womb, Jesus. Holy Mary, Mother of God, pray for us sinners, now and at the hour of our death. Amen.* That wind outside the cab swept the sidewalk of take-out trash and flyers and newspapers, even shook the padlocked wrought-iron grills and aluminum pull-downs. They got out under a scaffold walkway, X-braced on the street side, corrugated tin roof above. He found a glass door, a light on behind it making its color porcelain, this stained swirl of graffiti calligraphy decorating all equally, numbers blocked above it matching the address he'd gotten when he'd called an ad he'd read in the *Voice* — a cash-only bed-and-breakfast, way cheap, suspiciously available — and, her clutching him, he buzzed and it buzzed back and it was an office building, its inside the same city that was outside, and into an elevator door more like a ship, splintering wood flooring, black buttons. They took it to the top, the 8th, where it became an art gallery. Polished hardwood. Welded sculpture. Watercolor and oil paintings of broken naked men and naked women, smears of bodies, alone and together. Their room was a shape with no parallel sides and not the same length and the walls were painted different shades of orange and there were cheap Persian-style throw rugs and lead pipes to hang clothes on and a thick, tall picture window, too cold to touch, which framed images of buildings and lights in them and dark sky and they lay on a rolled-out futon on a straw mat.

Her breasts in his face, their flesh the butter of fantasy, the warm of sleep, her waist and hips the wafting curls of scent, her sighs not sounds but visual cues: love, woman. She was an instinctual shape, she was the innate and learned want of body pleasure, of want of tongue clitoris and nipple. She wanted to leak milk from her breasts like he did from his penis, and she sucked them with him and their saliva, mixed, stirred a juice, the essence of sweet, which became a hallucinogen transporting them into a heaven of space and a time both unremembered and always known but never visible, and they were man and woman, singular and pair. They were drenched in the spill of sweat and vagina and semen, all the slick inside of mythic womb that is private and protected, indescribable and familiar, its secret revealed, a mescaline calm, its absolute understanding in orgasm, rippling too in the mind like a contraction of birth, the squeezing and releasing, the mysterious desire and satisfaction of the egg and seed, of earth and God.

When they wandered out for a dinner it was a morning, not night, its gray the wet and dry dust of the city's sidewalks, its shine the silvery lead of scuffed grates and worn manhole covers, that storm of iced wind tossing crushed water bottles and even filtered cigarette butts but which this time only cooled them, bent their pacing. They walked, and they ate, and they went back into the ill-shaped room, now like a spring pasture, the stars reflections of windows in the high buildings across from them, where they became as blurred as oil paintings and then there was a cab and he wouldn't get out there with her but he saw her, the hat, the coat, the boots, walking away on the tiled *placita* under the sign that said MADISON SQUARE GARDEN.

Alonzo was from Lajoya, Texas, and he was seated at the bed-and-breakfast's table for ten, waiting for Vinika, who was from Philadelphia. She was a muscular big woman, and he was hungry thin and seemed taller than he really was. They had been staying in the room next door. Alonzo said he was a poet and an artist and now he was also doing Web design. Vinika killed cockroaches and rats for an extermination company. They'd met on the Internet. He'd started the communication with her through an African-American Women Only chat room. He laughed, looking up over the hand hiding his mouth as though it were a tall wall. When Vinika finished what she was doing, she stood next to Alonzo. A saggy, pocked suitcase was outside their room door, zipped up, a limp handle ready to be gripped. Alonzo had promised her the Trump Plaza, but the rooms were all sold out. It wasn't the money, he said, because he had the money. He only found this place at the last minute, it was the only thing available, the whole thing was the last minute. It was these holidays, he said. Vinika smiled as she stood next to Alonzo, though she wasn't looking at him. Then he got her bag and the two of them walked the long hall decorated with the unframed art to the elevator and then Alonzo was back.

We kind of heard you, Alonzo told him. Man! We plain out listened, like, you know, how couldn't we? Every little *cosita*. Vinika says to me, I want that, I want him. *Hijo de su!* You made me feel bad! She wouldn't do shit with me so we laid there hearing you two going, *pues* you know, sometimes whiles we was trying to sleep on these floor beds and then sometimes *también* when we're like waking up. I want that man, Vinika says to me. We were laughing sometimes, and *a veces* we just go like wow, those two are too much. Ay, when your woman camed out, down the hall, you know, to the bathrooms, a silky pink nightgown. *Hijole!* I'm sorry man, but she was fucking hotter than pink, a fucking killer *masota. Como* Raquel Welch, like that fine, good as la Salma. I'm thinking this dude, you know, *you*, like you gotta be some kinda movie star, or a rocker, or a *rico suave*, a *vato* who don't need to shine it up and that's why he's bad, some shit like that.

You two so fucking in love, *verdad? Se puede ver*, you can see how you're in love. And now you got no choice. You got to. Every dude, any dude. Yeah, you are fucked up now. She loves you too much, guy. She really loves you, and *que la fregada madre* you're screwed. It's like some movie. This is like some story out of fucking New York City!

They fast-walked its winter streets, a spin of dirty light, the squinty outdoors, as it bent and tweaked past the edges and over the tops of buildings and buildings. It was Alonzo talking, talking, and Geronimo sedated by the blows of her body against his—her lips wet, her eyes dazed—and numbed by images close and far, smaller and larger, distorting the new ones entering through his stunned sight.

Hey it's the Beats, man, and watch, Hettie Jones *es la mera mera. La* mommy of *vatos* like me, she's all hip mix Jew and Afro Nueva York. See I went over to her place because I found out where it was. It's what I camed here for reallys. Besides Vinika, who didn't know shit to care, man. And I yelled out her name, and *luego* she was like looking down out the window. She talked to me for reals, guy. Just talked at me, told both of us to come up into her crib, says I was doing good. You watch, cuz you'll see how she is. She convinced me like inspiration, meeting her is why I know I got my song now. See like if it weren't for the Beats, I wouldn't be knowing this shit and I wouldn't think *ni nada* about poetry and doing it. You gotta link the history, guy. It was probably *The Subterraneans* for me. I never been with no black girl neither, no black people in the Valley, you know what I'm saying, right, and that's what I was doing, with, you know, la Vinika. I was like all hot for an experience of her. Like she was gonna be saxophones, and trombones with those mutes, like jazz riffs and snapping fingers and little tiny espresso cups. But she like bombs rats! Which is even cooler, man, *verdad? También* funny! Gonna write it, guy, gotta write it. Poems, poetry! *El canto de Alonzo del valle*, that'll be the title. She was a tough *chingona* cookie, who didn't wanna give it up to me. *Ni modo.* I was afraid she was gonna kick my puny brown ass. You though, ay, it's gonna happen! I'm telling you. She loves you too much, so you better get used to it. I'm sorry to tell you, I'm sorry, brother, but I'm a truth-teller poet. Just think if she were an ugly! You're a lucky dude! You're gonna have a beautiful baby! And you love her too. I know you love her. Of course you love her.

"Never Montana, though once I was in Houston, but I've lived in Wyoming," Hettie Jones told him. Her smile seemed bigger than her apartment, too big for her body—she had to be the shortest person in the city.

"In some ways, yeah, Wyoming's like Montana," he said.

"I thought they were almost the same place."

"Everybody does, but they're not really. It's not just trees either, though I think Montana has more forest, more tall mountains."

"It's not like the Mexican border," she said.

160

"No ways," he said. "No cold like this ever. It's nothing like the desert, even when it gets cold."

"I liked being in Wyoming," she said, "but I didn't want to live there. It's not New York."

"It's not."

Jug wine was in chipped coffee mugs and he'd rolled what Alonzo had offered and that was almost done.

"She has to not have it."

"It's what I tell her," he said, "and it's like she's talking to somebody else on the phone."

Hettie said, "It'll be a mess. I went through this with Roi."

"It'll be done when I go up there to the clinic, near her home."

"You should have made her stay here," Hettie said. "You should've stayed with her until it was done."

"She said she had to go home first. I'm going up there to meet her."

"She's looking for a reason not to. There's no other explanation."

The blue lights that tipped the tallest buildings, the red ones that blinked under airplanes' wings, seemed as solitary in the heights as hawks and eagles and turkey vultures. The life that gripped beneath him and Hettie Jones and her tar-papered roof wailed sirens, car horns, and Bing Crosby's Christmas music.

"I don't feel real," he told her. "I never even thought of being here before."

"You're here, real or not," Hettie Jones said, shaking her head.

Hettie's friend, a millionaire and more, picked him up for a party in a black Lincoln Towncar, its pro driver wearing a billed hat. The millionaire was a handsome man with long hair the color of those intellectual wire glasses, and he wore jeans, which on him were classy — dry-cleaning clean and ironed — and his laugh was as glamorous as the woman beside him, and his lilting voice, both speedy and calm, too generous. A long black overcoat, a fabric with texture like a flower's petal, made him dressed. The woman leaned against him, a faint glow of bad in her blue eyes, a low-cut black gown that absorbed streetlight, which clung to her body in the way she didn't to him, so independent and willful in voice — she spoke Spanish to Geronimo with a Castilian accent. A suntan made her seem like she was a Californian but she was from so many places, it was hard to follow where she was from. She was on her way to the Hamptons for X and she was on her way to Miami for New Year's and then she was going to Paris but she had flown in from Monaco. The Hamptons were on Long Island, she explained, glancing at the millionaire. He told her where Geronimo was from and she nodded her head, intrigued. Really, she said.

In front of Elaine's restaurant, the millionaire and his date hugged and kiss-kissed the cheek of Robin Leach, the TV-show personality, who was getting into a white stretch limo. Geronimo politely shook his hand, too, before the chauffeur closed the door. He stayed behind the millionaire, his date going off on her own, when they went into the restaurant — it was just like the New York on TV and in movies — and a black tuxed maître d' sat them at a round table and they ordered drinks. Pat Riley, the basketball coach, was near the bar, and close to his ear he heard that that man standing there was a Kennedy, and so was that woman over there. As they sat down, he was introduced to the millionaire's friends, the owner Elaine, and Norman Mailer, who took the empty chair a few to Geronimo's left.

Mailer, pudgy and gray but a man who didn't seem to think of himself this way, elbowed into the pressed tablecloth holding a straight Scotch like it was a cigarette and asked Geronimo what he was doing in New York. Mailer nodded while Geronimo told him, and he was both sympathetic and unimpressed. Love, he said, was the only trouble that was worth the trouble, and of course it is as much raw instinct, the biochemistry of mating, simply not in your control. Mailer told the table he had just got back from Texas and Arizona and he asked Geronimo if he knew the writers there in El Paso, that McCarthy. It was a gunslinger question, like did he know John Wesley Harding. He answered that a man he'd just met, Alonzo, had introduced him to Hettie Jones here in New York. Mailer told the table he'd been out West only two weeks ago. Didn't seem to him there was anything of the east there, even though they try to import it like they did women a hundred years ago. I'd feel culturally abandoned there, he said. Mailer held back some before he asked him what he was. Geronimo took a second too. He'd always liked to tell people he was an Indian, but, just to see, he told this Mailer he was Mexican. But the name, Mailer asked, it's Native American? No, Geronimo told him, it's Spanish, it's because it's a Mexican name. Mailer didn't believe it entirely, but, to move along, asked Geronimo about his family. He said he was a father, and he had a wife, but, well. Mailer told him how many children and wives he'd had, and the table of men laughed, and so did Mailer, and he and Geronimo didn't say anything else to each other.

Yes, he told Hettie's friend, he wanted to leave the party too, he was ready to go. What he wanted was to get sleep and the next morning be on a bus. A few hours later, late afternoon, he wanted her to be waiting for him at the station. He wanted her to kiss him and he wanted to kiss her and wanted it to stay like that. He wanted them to go to her apartment where he would ask, only to be sure, if the appointment at the clinic was made. She had to make the appointment, she would have had to. She would have. It would be on the last day before it closed before Christmas, before that day baby Jesus was born, when the baby, when all babies, when all children are loved and given presents. He would have to reassure her. He would say, It has to be, and it is best, it will make us more happy, not less. He would hold her as he said this, his arm somewhere on her, in her hair, fingering her neck, or rubbing the little muscles in her shoulders. He would talk about love. He would talk about love and what would be. What they could do. What they would do. Together. He would be reassuring her, convincing her that it was the best thing, the right thing, the only thing, what love is, what it doesn't have to be, shouldn't and can't. He would go inside her when they went to bed and she would want him and they would make this love gently. In the morning they would be at the clinic. They would sit in those plastic orange waiting-room chairs, turning the crumpled pages in a *Good Housekeeping* magazine, seeing only smiley photos and happy food ads and positive headlines. There would be two more women there too, a young woman staring at *Ladies' Home Journal,* nondescript white blouse and no-brand blue jeans, who looked older than she was, with a mother or aunt, dark dress over her knees and black shoes, a flowery scarf over her head, both quiet and solemn. A dude with tattoos on the back of his hand, missing two fingers, and up his wrists and on his neck, and after she went in, saying nothing to him, this dude would start to talk to him. How this wasn't the first time he had to do this. How cold it was but you gotta smoke, how can you not smoke at least a cigarette, gotta go outside and not sit in there the whole goddamn time. Flocked stencils on the window outside of sleigh bells and stars and Santa and Rudolph the Reindeer. This dude would stand around with a strut even when he wasn't pacing, scanning, alert. This dude would be talking how where he came up, how when he came up, bragging and ashamed, how he didn't like being locked up but shit man, his baby, she's hard, and he's trying, he is trying to please the woman, don't you think he's trying to please the woman, chief? He's sure it's probably his. She wanted him to go here with her. She wanted me to. Like you, right, chief?

She was so tall she looked across at him directly in the eyes and she thumped her big chest right into his. She liked his cowboy boots. Said she liked his worn black jeans and that he was wearing that ordinary sweater. She put her palms against the sweater, pressing. She was drunk. She liked cowboys, or Indians. Or was he Latin? She liked him, she whispered, groping his arms. Her gray eyes were diamonds, her hair a gold fiber, she was as real as a magazine cover girl, a makeup or underwear or negligee ad. If he was not drunk, if he was not stoned, then what? She told him about Memphis. She'd lived in Memphis most of her life except when she'd lived in San Antonio and Germany. She loved San Antonio and missed it. She asked, Do you believe me, dollboy? He felt the heat of the whispered word "dollboy" as it struck his cheeks, lipstick-ad plump lips smearing him until she shoved her tongue into his mouth. Her girlfriends were laughing at her and when she stopped, she laughed overdramatically with them. Come on! she told him, and she held his hand staggering out of Elaine's restaurant and they were in the back of a cab. Her legs were across his lap and she pulled his hand under her coat and blouse and onto the crusty texture of her bra and while both her hands were on top of his, as though she were gasping for breath, she pushed his harder than he would have himself into her soft breasts, then pulled the bra above so that his fingers would strum her nipples.

Outside her apartment, under a darkened overhang at her building doorway, her leg was hooked around his so that she could rub against him, and her hand felt between his legs, tip to base. She was kissing his neck and he ran his hand on the wild curves of her impossibly perfect shape and though he was saying no he wanted to go up with her. How could he not but how could he, how could he, how this, now, her tongue licking his ears and neck, the smallest hairs tingling, him breathless. No, he kept telling himself. A couple of times he said, not very loud, no, he couldn't. He said it to himself and she didn't listen. Not out loud he told her about the pregnancy, love, children, and he was so afraid, and what would happen to him if this too? Not out loud he asked God what to do. Oh Mother of God, he said not out loud, and he saw Her, the Virgin, so beautiful, her eyes downward and shut, hands in prayer, those spikes of peaceful light warming and protecting her. Oh God, he said not out loud. She licked him. On the lips, on his nose, on his eyebrows, on his eyelids, rubbing his, rubbing hers against his thigh, his hand touching the skin of the tightest, smallest waist. Come upstairs and we'll take a bath, she said. Oh God no. No. When she heard him, she stopped, for that moment sober.

And there he was, back, lying on the futon, in the dark of the 8th floor room. Calm had begun to drizzle like a light rain. He missed his family, a wife and children, as though that were his own childhood, those Christmases, *luminarias* and *tamales dulces* and toys that were so meaningful that morning, Mass and bells and incense, the warmth that is sitting on a proch, seeing Mexico on the horizon, none of it going to be the same again, and then he missed all the land. That grizzly bear standing on his hind legs across a wide river in Glacier. He took himself out to Hueco Tanks, the Apache land outside El Paso, hiked up the rocks and sat where the always cooling wind whisked and the clouds drew in the sky. It got so still and quiet it made him see the plains in Wyoming, a herd of antelope grazing, far enough away from him, not so far. It took him a while to realize that he wasn't asleep, he wasn't dreaming. It was quieter than Wyoming. He got up and went to the big window, the one facing the buildings with column facades and fire-escape stairs, and he looked down on Broadway. It was white, snow so thick nothing passed, not a single car, van, or truck. Not even a taxi. Not a person. Not a sound. Not a bus. She was going to have a baby. Suddenly he saw a dog, an Irish setter, a leather leash hanging off its collar, leaping through the thick snow, hoops like stitches in a white cloth, barking joyous, the only sound out there now, barking, until in the frame, maybe ten feet behind the dog, a young woman, a cap, a jacket, a sweater, gloves, boots, every color that made him think of the sun, the West—green, red, yellow, orange, blue—chasing behind, losing ground, happy.

Note About the Artist

A native of Michoacán, Mexico, artist Artemio Rodríguez divides his time between Mexico City and Berkeley. His linocuts are also included in *Loteria Cards and Fortune Poems: A Book of Lives*. His handprinted books and prints, including a portfolio of "Woodcuts of Women," are available through his own press, Ediciones del Jorobado.